FLAME TO FROST

MYRA DANVERS

FOREWORD

Make sure you sign up for Myra's Newsletter so you never miss sexy NSFW art, free things, exclusive deals, and loads of other cool shit you do not want to miss...

Sign up for Myra's Newsletter today!

myradanvers.com/mailing-list

This book is dedicated to the original Lit crowd.
Those who hate change enough to pester me about this
version of Mila and Asher every day for the last four years
because, "I liked the new version, I guess, but the old
version was better/incredible/special and I will pay any
amount of money to get my hands on the original!!"

Fine, okay? FINE. You win. Here it is. Lightly edited, a
couple of scenes added for extra spice (I'm legit proud of
the smexy scene at the end of this one, mmkay? ;P), but
this is the original cult classic in all its fledgling author
glory.
The alternate version of this book is now listed under the
series name: Tritan Evolution.
Enjoy, and I love you all. <3

1

———

But first, an important note from the author

This is book one in the series, *The Last Tritan.* It is not to be confused with the series called *Tritan Evolution*, though they share many similarities. Which is confusing, I know. There's an explanation coming, and I'm going to try to make it as straightforward as I can.

I cut my authorling teeth in a weird little corner of the internet called Literotica. It's a place where free dirty stories go to flourish or die, based on the reception from what can be accurately and fairly called *"a snake pit of anonymous readers."* Free stories in exchange for brutal honesty.

The Last Tritan—in its original form—dominated the top ten of the top fifteen spots in Literotica's Hall of Fame for the category I was listed in. Which is absolutely a humble brag, but I also worked really hard to get there and I'll never forget how I got my start. I had ambition that went beyond publishing free stories, and it wasn't long before I took the whole thing down and rewrote it.

The original story (which begins with this book, *Flame to Frost, The Last Tritan, book I*) is a thing I never thought would see the light of day again. In fact, I went out of my way to dodge requests for the original story for years before I realized...

For the people who read the first, raw version of Mila and Asher... there was something bitter sweet about losing the bulk of the original story to the editing bin, no matter how proud I am of Tritan Evolution. Nostalgia is real, and the two versions of Tritan are so different from each other that they can exist on the same bookshelf without one smothering the other.

So this is it. The ORIGINAL version of The Last Tritan. Gritty, raw, and with a few never before seen bonus scenes sprinkled in. It is utterly different from its successor, *Ravenous Innocence, Tritan Evolution, Book I.*

They can be read separately, as they are essentially very different stories that merely share similar elements.

Thank you for reading, and enjoy.

Myra Danvers

I was eighteen when the capital city of Tritan fell.

With the element of surprise on their side, the fight was relatively bloodless and over within a week. They crushed our communication network, and it was days before we even knew who our attackers were. Once we saw the black-and-gold banners of Caledonia, however, our self-defense attempts were virtually nonexistent—they were known for being ruthless in battle. It was assumed the Caledonians had attacked Tritan for her abundant resources. And it was true—to an extent.

With the government disabled, mass panic quickly followed. Families trying desperately to escape the tattered carcass of Tritan fled to the northern country of Elora, but only found doors slammed shut in their faces. The Elorans were terrified of incurring the wrath of Caledonia.

They were right to fear.

Our enemy had more than a reputation for blood lust—their elite soldiers could channel energy into the weapons they carried. Specially modified guns that fired blasts of pure energy hot enough to burn through anything it encountered made for deadly warriors, unmatched in any known arena.

The true horror of our invasion had yet to be revealed. Renowned for our genteel natures, slight statures, light hair, and fair complexions, our people were valued for our contributions to medical sciences and bountiful food production. For our peacekeepers and healers.

And for our priestesses.

Tritan women who could feel the energy of every organic thing around them. Who could manipulate life by reshaping it as something new—trees, plants, animals—*anything* that held a spark of living energy. Priestesses were famous healers, using their abilities to detect and diagnose ailments in their patients. But the most powerful could direct that energy to heal any injury.

As medics, they might have been invaluable on the battlefield. Might have given our scattered forces a whisper of hope against Caledonia's elite warriors.

But the temple was the first to fall.

The true target of Caledonia's attack, for, by some cruel stroke of fate, the Caledonians could enslave the priestesses in chains of glittering gold. Bound to one of these elite warriors, Tritan's cherished holy women were nothing more than conduits to the world's living energy. Taken by the conquerors who came to enslave, to use until there was nothing left but an empty husk. Tritan burned, and from her smoldering corpse, the enemy rose in a cloud of ash.

Invincible.

Limitless power at their disposal.

There was no chance of a rebellion after that.

But it wouldn't be a story worth telling if it ended there. I escaped the city before the fighting reached us because my father used his position as a senator to get me to safety. Just as he'd done years before, when my modest talents as a potential priestess had begun to manifest. Forbidding me from honing my craft—from wasting my life in selfless worship—was a biased decision that eventually saved my life. Unfortunately, he couldn't secure the same for himself and my mother.

It was the last time I saw them.

Some of Tritan's refugees managed to find a temporary haven in the vast forest separating Tritan and Elora. Not rebels—just desperate people trying to avoid the nets of those hunting them. I was among those small clusters of terrified people, and though I never met another priestess, it became obvious the Caledonians wanted even the ordinary citizens of Tritan. Our unusual coloring made us highly sought after in the slaving markets across the world.

It wasn't long before slavers invaded the woods. Before they attacked.

Drawn in by the ignorance of those who knew nothing of survival in the forest and even less of the stealth needed to escape unnoticed.

Late one evening, I awoke to the scent of meat roasting over a fire. Serenaded by the merry sounds of popping and crackling flames. One of the men had brought down some type of fowl and had started a fire to cook it. The smell of roasted bird soon woke the remaining sleepers, and although we knew better, it was a temptation none could resist.

There was only enough for each of us to have a few mouthfuls of the succulent meat, but as the hot juices dripped off our fingers, I was sure it was worth it—until the slavers crashed through the brush, weapons drawn. The camp sounds, which moments before had been contented eating, became screams of terror as everyone scrambled for safety.

It was my first good look at the dreaded Caledonians.

Where Tritans were slight and fair, the Caledonians were the opposite. Dark hair and eyes with considerably larger, heavily muscled frames.

I had but a moment to make this observation before my impending enslavement became apparent. I was a Tritan priestess, albeit an untrained one, and I couldn't allow myself to fall into the clutches of an elite warrior to be used against my people in such a perverse way.

To my everlasting shame, I took the opportunity the chaos offered and slipped away. I knew I wouldn't have long before the slavers finished subduing my countrymen, so I took to the trees. The largest branches were thick enough to jump from one to the other, effectively allowing me to distance myself from any incriminating trails.

Safe in a delicate network of branches, where no

bulky Caledonian might follow.

I had a head start, and I wouldn't waste it. After I had almost fallen to my death, I slept the rest of that first night huddled inside a hollow log. I awoke the next morning with bugs crawling all over my skin, tangled in my hair. As it turned out, sleeping in a rotting log was far from the cleanest place I could have chosen.

Pushing aside my revulsion, I brushed away as many insects as I could while listening for any sounds that could be out of place in the silence of the forest. Thankfully, I could hear nothing, so I carefully crawled from my hiding place into the brisk chill of early morning.

I quickly realized I faced more problems than evading capture. If I didn't find a reliable food source, I would likely starve to death before the long winter months. Heavy rainfall was a daily occurrence, so water was not an issue. Being raised with the privilege of being a politician's daughter, I had never lacked fresh meat and vegetables, though I was certainly feeling it now. As far as I knew, starving to death wasn't even the worst of my problems. If I didn't have access to fresh fruit with vitamin C, I could develop scurvy or other issues.

With no option but to deal with one thing at a time, I fashioned a snare for trapping a small animal. I had seen plenty of squirrels and rabbits as I made my plans. I just needed to catch one.

It was three days before I managed to trap anything. By then, I was weak with hunger and spent most of my time sleeping. With a detached certainty, I knew I didn't have much time before I wouldn't be able to drag my tired body to safety if the slavers found me. But to my immense satisfaction, I had a plump rabbit caught in my snare within a few hours of those dreadful thoughts.

All I had to do was kill the fluffy little thing. Placing the blade of my knife at the soft throat, I braced for the kill.

I should have closed my eyes.

Shouldn't have looked into the inky black depths of an innocent creature's terrified gaze. Of their own accord, my fingers began stroking soft brown fur, soothing it. Its little heart beat so fast against my palm that I began to worry it would die from fright in my hands, when I ought to have been eager for its death.

And with a whispered apology, my grip loosened, and I let it go.

I'd showed mercy to an animal that would have made my existence much easier. But when I'd gazed into those beautiful dark eyes and saw the absolute terror I had recently had a taste of, I felt a certain kinship with the captured rabbit.

And I'd failed to push the blade through its soft fur to take its life.

I still faced imminent starvation, and now I was

without the strength to check my remaining snares. The chance to change my mind had passed with a breath of mercy.

I collapsed onto the forest floor, staring up at the thick foliage and squirrels as they raced along their treetop highways.

This was the end.

But as I lay there, I noticed the tree above had large green fruits hanging from its branches. Though I didn't recognize them, malnutrition had a funny way of making one keen to try anything. Glancing around, I realized there were several of the fruits scattered across the forest floor. The squirrels certainly seemed to enjoy them, so I hoisted myself off the ground and reached for one. After all, I was beyond the point of caring if I died from eating a poisonous plant.

I bit into the green husk and promptly retched— the flavor and texture made it clear the thing was not for eating. Hurling the offensive fruit against the nearest tree in disgust, I watched with detachment as the green husk exploded, leaving behind an ovular black pit. Frowning, I crawled over to the palm-sized pit for a closer inspection.

"A walnut," I whispered, excitement lending me the energy to find two rocks. Knowing it was edible, I bashed the walnut into smithereens in my enthusiasm. Gleefully picking the pieces out of the shell, I stuffed the 'meat' into my mouth, knowing walnuts were jam-packed with nutrients, proteins, fat, and vitamins and would keep well during the winter months.

At the very least, I knew they would keep me alive.

I spent most of the day collecting walnuts and throwing them against trees to remove the husks. Touching them with my bare hands produced a dark brown stain that no amount of washing could remove. But what did I care about dirty hands when I now had a food source? One that would keep well without spoiling, that I could store for months and eat well even in the winter.

It was time to find shelter.

I decided to take inspiration from the wildlife that thrived, where I could barely take a step without blundering it in some way or another. So, I sat and watched the squirrels and rabbits for the better part of a day, hardly daring to move for fear of disturbing them from their regular habits. I observed as they ate some plants and avoided others, stored food for the coming winter, and fattened themselves on the forest's bounty.

Most importantly, I watched as the squirrels darted in and out of their homes, hidden in the very hearts of the trees. My face cracked in the first genuine smile I'd had since the horror of the invasion.

I had a plan.

2

———

Wandering the forest, always heading in the opposite direction of the soldiers at my back, I searched for a tree. It had to be a magnificent grandmother tree, one so old and large that I wouldn't be able to see the top or wrap my hands around the middle. After days of searching, I finally came across the perfect specimen —an oak tree older than living memory by several generations. It was so large that its canopy blocked out the sun, creating the illusion of dusk at high noon. Some branches reached far into the space of neighboring trees, while others brushed the ground, having bowed under their weight after hundreds of years of life.

If there was a more perfect tree in all the forest, I hadn't found it in days of searching.

Climbing into the massive arms of my new home,

I settled in and began to dig. In the crook of the oak tree, I chipped away until I'd carved a shallow indentation—enough space for me to sleep unseen, albeit curled in a ball. I became utterly obsessed with making the perfect hideaway, and I spent my time tediously digging out a small room.

It was nearly winter before I finished, and I had just enough time to create a trapdoor for the roof. I included several virtually invisible windows to be used as ventilation shafts for small fires when the cold of winter settled in. An invaluable advantage should someone try to sneak up on my location.

Burning walnut shells produced a brilliant, hot flame with little smoke. A cheap source of heat, a small stone fireplace, and the perfect fuel source— with my trap door and tight sleeping quarters, I had created a cozy little winter-proof nook.

Over the next two years, my life was a testament to survival. Every day I remained free was a blessing and each new skill I mastered was a treasure. I made flour out of acorns, created my clothing, expanded my tree apartment, and created a virtual highway in the tree-tops—though I never shared my paradise with anyone.

Three major events played a role in defining who I'd become. The latter two spawned from the meeting of one small, battered family. Winter had just set in, and I'd spent the summer hollowing out two more trees for use as food storage. On my way back from the closer tree, I saw a ragged group of dark-haired people with olive skin. There were four, all throwing wild-eyed glances over their shoulders.

Refugees.

Hunted like chattel.

But I had learned the risks of exposure the hard way.

Pushing aside the instant kinship I felt, I immediately tried to slip away unseen. I knew the danger of traveling in large groups—that the lure of safety was a treacherous thing that would only draw unwanted attention.

Slavers.

In my haste, I stepped on a branch, the crunch louder than thunder to the fugitives below me. Frozen, I could barely draw breath, terrified they would see me in the shadows.

"Father! There's someone in the trees," a girlish voice whispered.

After a moment, a man interrupted the silence of the clearing. "Hello? Can you help us?" he asked, his despair evident. "Please?"

My mouth opened, but nothing came out. After I cleared my throat, I tried again. "Who are you?" Brilliant first words. But my head was spinning, and my hands trembled with the need to end this conversation and flee.

"My name is Jake Trapper, and this is my family.

Please, Elora has been invaded, and the slavers are after us. We need help. Please, you have to—"

"Elora?" I said, taking a step forward, shocked.

"She's a Tritan," the woman all but shrieked, speaking for the first time, her voice shrill in the silence of the clearing.

"Miss, have you been in the forest since Tritan fell?" Jake asked, taking a tentative step in my direction, clearly just as surprised as I was. When I didn't answer, he rushed forward. "You have to teach us how to survive here—please. Save my children!"

My eyes widening in surprise, I stumbled back, my feet catching on scattered branches. Feeling the world tilt, I flung out my hands, reaching for anything that might restore my balance. Fingernails clawing at the tree bark.

Jake continued as though I hadn't nearly fallen from the tree. "We can help you! You have to see that." His eyes filled with tears.

"I-I can't, sir. I don't know—" I stammered, crumbling under the pressure.

"Just some food and water. Please?"

It was a trap.

A trap loaded with the dirty, tear-stained faces of his children.

"Stay hidden," I said after a long pause before melting into the foliage. My survival instincts screamed this was a mistake. Helping these people would make me vulnerable, and it was my freedom on the line.

It would be nothing to disappear in the forest and never see them again… but that was a mistake I'd made once before. One that haunted my dreams.

"Here," I murmured as I re-emerged from the semi-dark canopy. I dropped a handmade bag, stuffed full of nuts and acorn bread, at his feet. "There's a small stream just through this clearing. Walk through there," I said, pointing. "You can't miss it."

His children fell on the bag immediately, stuffing bits of bread into their mouths while cracking walnuts.

"Thank you," Jake said, pressing his hand to his heart.

"I don't have enough food stored up to feed every-one," I warned.

"Teach me," he said, holding eye contact.

In the face of his determination to survive, I could do nothing except agree. I nodded. "Find somewhere to sleep tonight," I said and turned to leave.

"Take us with you!" the woman screamed.

I dropped to my stomach, arms and legs clinging to the branch in fear. After a few moments of desper-ately listening for the sounds of approaching slavers, I glared at the hysterical idiot. "Control yourself," I hissed, anger making my thin veil of civilization disappear.

Jake moved to put a hand on the woman's arm. "Tomorrow?" he asked, his eyes begging me to forgive her.

"I'll find you," I said and fled. It was winter—I had no idea how these people expected me to keep them alive with no food, but I decided to try.

In the morning, I traversed my treetop highway until I returned to the place they had been. I could track them easily from the trees, so I had no doubt the slavers would find it even easier to hunt them down.

"Lesson one," I said, descending from my perch, my feet touching the ground for the first time in at least a week. "They can track you easily through the snow—cover your tracks." I demonstrated as their eyes followed my every movement.

"Your clothes are funny," the youngest boy said, plucking at my pants.

"I made them," I said, more than a little uncomfortable with his proximity.

Jake pulled his son closer. "Do they keep you warm?"

"Very, but I keep moving most of the day—especially when it's really cold," I replied, fidgeting.

Luckily, they all appeared to be dressed for the weather—it had taken me months of trial and error to create the rough wool-like cloth I now wore as a sweater. I'd made it from strips of well-worn plant fibers and the threads of my old clothing. My pants were even more unique, fashioned from large chunks of tree bark and my original pants' remains. I looked like a crazy, battle-ready forest nymph, and I knew it.

"Tell me about the war," I said abruptly, wanting some give and take from our relationship.

"Well, after Tritan fell, we knew Elora was next. The Empire of Caledonia has been forcibly taking over countries for years now—we didn't think they would come as far north as Tritan and Elora. We're peaceful, developed countries, for God's sake, and we've never had problems with the Caledonians before." He paused to eat some dried berries from the fresh bag I had brought before continuing. "Tritan fell so quickly that we didn't have a chance to help, but it gave us time to shore up our defenses." He shrugged, a bitter pinch between his brows. "Didn't make much of a difference. Their elites used your priestesses like supercharged batteries, and they've spent a good amount of time developing new weapons. They're unstoppable." When I grimaced, he apologized, though he couldn't have known the cause of my discomfort. "We left before they took the capital, and we've been running ever since."

"How long?" I asked.

"About a week."

It was my turn to frown. Assuming the slavers would be busy rounding up the Elorans still within the city, we would have some time before they came searching for this ragged little family and others like them. Time enough to get them to safety if I were lucky and the weather held.

"So how about you?" he asked, taking another mouthful from his pile of food. "What's your name? How long have you been in these woods?"

"I think that's enough for today," I said, standing abruptly. After so much time alone, I was extremely uncomfortable around others and had no desire to talk about my most horrific memories. I practically launched myself into the trees in my haste to get away from the offer of friendship in Jake's eyes. Friends died, and I couldn't afford the risk of caring for these people only to lose them to slavers or starvation.

Almost against my will, I found myself returning daily, hungry for the knowledge and companionship they offered. I brought them food every day, greatly depleting my stores until they figured out how to trap their own animals.

About a week after meeting them, I arrived in their camp just as Jake was gutting and cleaning a rabbit. My stomach lurched at the bloody sight, and I felt a little piece of my heart crumble in sadness at the waste of life. Though I couldn't expect Jake to let his family starve to death, I was still repulsed by his actions.

"Join us for dinner," he said gleefully, holding up the bloody, skinless carcass of the rabbit. I felt the blood drain from my face, and I took an involuntary step back.

"No, thank you," I said in barely more than a whisper. Frowning upon seeing my reaction, he shook his head.

"You Tritans are soft-hearted, aren't you?" he asked with a genuine smile.

"I tried to kill a rabbit once. Couldn't do it," I said, laughing nervously.

"Well, I've done it this time, and you're more than welcome to join us. Please, it's the least we can do in return for all your help," he said, walking toward their makeshift shelter, careful to cover his tracks. I shrugged.

"How could I justify eating it if I am incapable of killing it? It hardly seems fair to benefit from its death if I don't have the courage to end its life," I said, trying for the first time to voice my discomfort with eating flesh.

"Eloquently put," he exclaimed as we entered the campsite. "So, are you a priestess?"

"No," I replied, unable to make eye contact, though I wasn't strictly lying. I was never accepted into the temple and had no formal training.

"No, I don't suppose there are any left. None who aren't chained to an elite, that is." My head bowed in sadness. Excluding me, he was probably right. "Anyway, we can't stay in these woods forever. We heard there's a safe passage to cross the ocean if we can make it to the coast. You should join us."

I offered a benign smile, not committing to anything.

"Are you ever going to tell me your name, or do I have to keep talking in your general direction?"

Going still, I watched Jake from beneath lowered lashes. Inspecting him, but for what, I didn't know. Couldn't name.

Amusement lit his face, and I took a moment to wonder at my hesitation in revealing my name. It wasn't like his knowing could harm me in any way I could think of—so what was it then? Assuming it must have been my reluctance to let people get close to me, I staunchly pushed aside my discomfort and took a deep breath.

"Mila." My voice was hardly more than a whisper, and Jake's head snapped around in surprise to look at me.

"You've been helping us for weeks. I wasn't expecting you ever to tell me. Mila is a beautiful name. Thank you." He rested his hand on my shoulder. I nodded and touched his hand, realizing it was the first time in almost two and a half years that I had had skin-to-skin contact, however fleeting. Rhonda came out of the woods, an angry look already on her face.

"Jake, come here! I need you," she called in her shrill voice, glaring at my hand touching his. Sighing, Jake obediently walked toward his furious wife. Sending more than one weighted glance in my direction, they had a terse, angry conversation, but with my patience worn too thin, I retreated to the trees.

I headed back to my treetop apartment, then settled in for the night. There was no room in my life for a partner, especially not the kind who came with two kids and a jealous wife. I drifted off, wondering what Jake had done to inspire such hostility in his wife.

The morning chill woke me, and I treated myself to a leisurely breakfast of roasted acorn bread with dried berries and warm water. It might not sound like much, but I was damn proud of my survival skills. In the entire time I'd lived here, I hadn't seen a single other person manage to do the same.

I took my time heading back to Jake's camp, enjoying the refreshing winter air. Hearing voices, I frowned. I was still a five-minute walk away, which meant they weren't making any effort to remain hidden. This I couldn't understand—silence had been lesson two.

Crouching in the trees, I advanced as quietly as possible. The realization I didn't recognize the voices hit me quite suddenly. My blood went cold.

Slavers.

Hoping there might still be some chance to save them, I crept closer. The cloying flavor of fear clung to the back of my throat, but I pressed close enough to hear the conversation taking place beneath me.

"I had to sedate the woman. Screeching about

Tritans running through the trees like squirrels. Ha! I haven't seen a Tritan in a year, the idiot." His voice was gruff and suited his massive frame perfectly.

The second man laughed as he picked at one of my 'care packages' filled with walnuts and home-made bread. He took a bite. "Bleh! This shit is awful," he said, spitting the offensive bread in the direction of his four bound prisoners. "You'll be happy with your new masters—they won't feed you anything half as bad as *that*." He laughed and kicked at the fire smoldering in the center of the camp.

I grimaced. Lesson three had been *no unprotected fires*. The smoke must have brought these two down on this little family almost as quickly as it had been lit. They must have lit a fire to cook the rabbit and not bothered with all the tricks I'd taught them.

"Please, you can't do this to my children. Have a heart," Jake said, voice cracking brokenly.

I shifted so I could see him, and found a man who'd been savagely beaten. The left side of his face was swollen, and there was an ominous dark stain on the back of his neck that looked too much like blood for my comfort.

As the big slaver stalked closer to his prisoners, I took the opportunity to move in the trees, preparing for an attack. If I could drop down on top of the smaller one, I could knock him out and would do my best to subdue the giant. Either way, I was tired of doing nothing.

Muscles coiled tight and ready to pounce, I hesitated just long enough to be struck with heartbreak.

"There's a Tritan in these woods!" Jake shouted, trembling. His palms raised in a wasted effort to ward off another blow. "I swear it! Free my wife and children, and I'll help you find her."

The big man guffawed as he hoisted Jake up by his coat. "Take me to this mystery Tritan first, and then we'll talk."

"Her name is Mila, and she made that bread. She's been living here since Tritan fell. Please, she's been helping us, and she visits every day. She must live close to here. You have to believe me!"

Jake's captors were not sympathetic to his cries. There was a loud crack, and Jake slumped unconscious against his wife. His children sobbed pitifully until they, too, were sedated.

"If there were a Tritan hiding in these woods, she'd be worth a fortune. Probably the last free Tritan in the world," the smaller slaver said. "It would be nice to knock old Allister off his pedestal," he said with a dreamy quality to his voice.

Completely uninterested in whoever this Allister was, I let my thoughts drift back to the betrayal I had just witnessed. Angry that Jake could turn on me after all the help I had given him—and so easily! Hurt pumped through my chest, leaving me cold. Frigid and still, I waited until the slavers began to pack up their wares, hoping there might be enough noise to cover my exit.

Reckless as I ran through the trees, I let my anger stew. I seethed until the tear-streaked faces of Jake's children flashed before my eyes, and I skidded to a halt.

Jake was a man who would do anything to protect his family.

A choked sob escaped my throat, surprising me. Tears? For someone who had just betrayed me? But I knew in my heart I would have done the same thing if it meant I could have saved my parents.

Had I made a mistake in not staying to help the Trapper family? Of course I had. If I couldn't fight to save my fellow humans, then why was I struggling so hard to survive? It all seemed like a huge waste of effort if I couldn't do any good with my life. Turning on my heel, I backtracked as quickly as possible, though my attempts to remain quiet slowed my progress. By the time I returned to the remains of the camp, they were gone.

It wasn't hard to track them through the snow, as slavers never bothered to hide their passing. I followed as quickly as possible until I could hear travelers in the forest. My only chance at a rescue would come at night when everyone was sleeping. Hanging back, I waited for my chance.

I'd learned most of what I knew about survival by watching the animals, but it was through trial and

error that I realized my digestive system was funda-
mentally different from a bird's. That not all berries
were safe, despite the avian feeding frenzies I'd
observed and the pleasant, if bitter, aftertaste.

It was a lesson learned from a night curled in the
fetal position, vomiting until I was sure I had cracked
a rib. So consumed with my misery, I couldn't so
much stand on legs that trembled and quaked.

But a lesson, nevertheless.

One that could be put to more sinister purposes,
for as I trailed behind the captured Trapper family, I
noticed a tree laden with the last of the summer's
horrid little red berries. Dry and thoroughly picked
over by the birds, but whispering a plan of action.

When night fell, I waited on the outskirts of the
slaver's camp, as far away from the Trappers as I
could manage—if one of the children saw me and
called out, the game would be up.

When the larger of the two slavers went to sleep, I
threw a rock into the forest as hard as possible. It
bounced off a tree, and the remaining slaver's head
snapped up. He stared in the direction of the sound
for so long that I feared he wouldn't get up to check.

"Probably just an animal," he said absently as he
walked toward the opposite side of the clearing.

Dropping from my lofty perch on silent feet, I
hurried to the camp coffee simmering over the fire,
dumped the powdered red berries into the pot,
stirred, then retreated to the darkness to wait.

When the smaller slaver woke his partner for the change of guard, I waited long enough to watch them each drain a mug of coffee before I drifted off to sleep.

Dawn was breaking when I heard the musical sounds of retching. Two of the largest men I had ever seen in my life, taken down by a simple fruit. The red berries earned their place as a force to be reckoned with and a feature spot in my arsenal against the Empire.

Creeping across their campsite, I looted the small man's prone body for the keys to the Trapper's restraints. He didn't react when my hand brushed his skin, so I slipped the keys out of his pocket, moving as slowly as possible.

The Trappers were all staring wide-eyed at me, and both parents had their hands pressed to the children's mouths. I unlocked the two adults, handed the keys to Rhonda, and then motioned for Jake to follow me.

"Follow my lead," I whispered, handing him a set of cuffs. Cautious of startling the smaller slaver out of his nausea-induced stupor, I gently took each of his wrists in my hand and chained them together. Jake did the same with the other, who had woken up long enough to swear at Jake and continue vomiting.

"Mila, I—"

"Stop," I said, anger bubbling to the surface. "I want nothing more to do with you, traitor. Take your family and run to the coast. Don't stop until you get there. I think it's about a day's hike from here. These two will be sick for the next day or two, so you'll have a head start. Don't waste it." Turning to leave, I glanced at Jake and his family over my shoulder. "Take care of each other."

"Thank you, Mila," Rhonda said, her voice stiff.

I didn't bother looking back.

3

————

As aloof as I tried to seem, I knew the Trapper family would stay with me for a long time. I'd fought hard to save them, and I took several important things away from my first slaver experience.

The Tritans—my people—had become a rare commodity, and slavers would do just about anything to get their hands on me.

And I was tired of hiding. Of watching from the trees and learning how best to be alone. If I could make life just a little harder for the Caledonians, maybe I could make amends for the Tritans I'd abandoned when we first took refuge in the forest.

But if I looked like a Tritan, I would surely become a target. On the other hand, if I looked like an Eloran, I would be nothing more than a nuisance.

An enemy of the state who'd be given no mercy for the crimes I planned to commit.

The answer was simple. It had been staining my hands a dark, unwashable brown from the first days of my life in the forest.

Walnuts.

It took longer than I thought it would, but I eventually developed a walnut soak for my hair that turned it a rich, dark brown. The dye only lasted about three washes, but no one would be the wiser if I were diligent with the upkeep. The only downside to constantly staining my hair was the mess it made of my skin.

Blotchy up to my elbows, the stains covered much of my face and neck. It wasn't permanent, and, without a mirror, my vanity withered on the vine. Now more than ever, I looked like a crazy nature spirit.

I began to actively seek out the slavers, freeing many of their captive Elorans. Though I wasn't sure how many found freedom, I was able to give them a second chance—an opportunity my father had bought with his life.

But although I rescued dozens of fugitive Elorans, I was never bold enough to risk exposing myself again. Jake had been my friend, and he would have slapped the chains on me himself if given half a chance. It was better to take the temptation out of their way.

Better to be alone.

News of Elora was never encouraging. They were losing the war, and the Caledonians managed to strike down any rebellion attempts before they had truly begun. Most tried to take their families and run, which brought more slavers to the forest. More refugees and dirty, hungry children with sad eyes and desperate parents.

Aside from the new risk, my life settled into a predictable pattern—wake up, scavenge for food, find slavers, poison them with red berries, and free their slaves.

But patterns bred predictability, and I was not immune. The slavers began to swap stories of drinking bitter coffee, sharing whispers of the foul creature that would emerge from the gloom of the canopy to steal their wares. An evil spirit whose very presence brought a plague of uncontrollable vomiting and empty coin purses.

When the slavers began traveling in larger groups, it became clear that I needed a new trick in my fight against the empire.

A trick I'd been born with. One I'd been forbidden to use, but could no longer afford to ignore.

As long as one priestess was fighting for Tritan, for Elora, the war was not lost.

Searching my brain for inspiration, I recalled the beautiful male mountain lion I had seen earlier in the year. Thankfully, he had just made a kill and wasn't interested in me, but I did manage to get a good look at the frightening length of his teeth.

I had my muse and endless, idle hours to play the mimic.

I survived for another few years in the forest, freeing slaves and thwarting their hunters. Watching, fighting alone as the seasons began to blend, and I lost track of time altogether.

The sound of screaming woke me early one morning. Before I had taken the time to eat breakfast, I was racing through the trees, determined to help. A pouch of powdered red berries on my left hip, a satchel of acorn flatbreads on the other.

When I found them, I came upon men taunting two women bound to a tree. Crude, their hands wandering where they had no ownership, pinching and taking liberties.

Seething, I employed my usual tricks to distract the men so I could dose their coffee. To my relief, they fell for the conspicuous sound in the woods as easily as the others, and I crept into their camp to work my dark magic on the coffee. Dumping the entire pouch in a fit of frayed nerves and sparkling temper.

And so, when both slavers started vomiting a mere twenty minutes after drinking the coffee, I thought nothing of it. Merely slipped into camp and lifted the keys. Both women eyed me with a mixture of what appeared to be shock and disgust—I guessed my appearance was about as far away from comforting as possible.

But I eyed them with an equal amount of shock, for these were the most statuesque Elorans I'd ever seen—both with inky dark hair and long, lean muscles.

These were women worthy of friendship!

"I'm here to help," I whispered, showing them the keys in my hand. The one closer to me nodded and held out her wrists, which I unlocked with nimble fingers before moving to the other.

"Thank you," they said together, and I flashed a toothy smile. One never seen before, that evoked slack-jawed awe, for I'd put my modest priestess skills to use.

All four of my canines had been made to grow pointed and long. Not the full six-inch glory of a mountain lion's impressive weaponry, but enough to see these women blanch white with shock.

"Are you the one who's been freeing slaves?" the closer woman asked, giving her head a shake as she reached out to touch my arm.

I stepped out of her grasp, offering a wary nod.

She smiled, then. And it was sharp. Confident. "Good."

A fist slammed into my ribs, drawing a startled yelp from my lips. Stealing my breath.

But the sound of cracking ribs was secondary to

the deep, masculine voice that suddenly filled my ears. "Welcome to the party. We've been waiting a long time for you."

"God, she's a mess. This disgusting little thing has been causing all the trouble?" a female said as my baffled gaze darted to the women I had just freed. They stood with feet shoulder-width apart, checking cruel-looking weapons.

A trap.

One I'd ignored in my haste to rescue women from abuse.

Women who stood with all the impressive height and stature of a full-blooded Caledonian warrior.

Gut clenching, I scrambled to my feet. Trying to ignore the crippling pain in my ribs, I made a mad dash for the tree line.

Two huge hairy arms wrapped around me before I'd made it ten feet, snaring me in a circle of crushing muscle.

With a yelp, I sank my modified teeth into the wiry forearm closest to my chin and didn't let go until I tasted blood.

A colorful curse spattered against my cheek, but his grip loosened enough for me to pull free.

I hadn't taken more than twenty steps before I heard a whistle and crack of screaming, splitting air.

It took longer to feel it.

Blinding pain snapped across my back from shoulder to hip. I couldn't remember hitting the ground, but I recalled the agony of my arm being wrenched behind my back.

"Don't you fucking move!" a male shouted in my ear, as if I could go anywhere with his weight pinning me to the forest floor.

"Little bitch bit me," the other man snarled from somewhere off to my left. "Look at these teeth marks! Fuck!" A moment later, there was a hand in my filthy hair, yanking my head up. My stunned gaze met the eyes of the furious man I'd bitten. Without warning, his fingers were pushing past my lips, running over my gums. Dirty fingernails scored the inside of my lip.

I snapped my teeth closed on his thumb.

"Nice try," he hissed, then jammed half his fist in my mouth, putting so much pressure on my jaw that it was impossible to retaliate. "Look at these teeth!"

"You'd better get a shot when we get back. No telling what she's got," the contemptuous voice of one of the women muttered as the fist was removed from my mouth.

"Did you guys drink the coffee? She poisoned it," the other woman said, kicking me.

"Nah," said the man whose knee was working to turn my bones into pulp. Who backed off only when his knee slipped in the blood oozing from my whip lash, wrenching my arm high between my shoulder blades.

"Pl—" I gasped, trying to force a breath through

the pain, and failed. Head spinning as blood ran freely down my sides and pooled at my front.

"Here, little kitty," she purred, bringing the pot of coffee to my lips.

"Eww, Tasha. Don't. She's going to be puking for hours. And if we believe the stories, it'll come from both ends. I'm *not* cleaning that up," the other woman said as she wound her whip. How I could feel grateful to the beast who had just laid open my back, I couldn't understand.

"Pack up. There's an auction tonight," the man restraining me said after he'd bound my wrists and ankles and dragged me to my feet. My legs wouldn't support my weight, which didn't seem to be a problem as he slung me over his shoulder. Ignoring the wet wheeze he forced from my lips as my ribs protested.

The wetness seeping through my shirt.

The man I had bitten appeared in my line of sight, then stuffed a filthy rag in my mouth. "I'll let your new owner decide what to do with those teeth," he said, smiling with a cruel glint in his eyes. As brave as I was trying to be, I couldn't help the frightened whimper—and the grunts of pain—as we started the hike through the woods.

4

———

It took the better part of the day to reach a road. I was sure I lost consciousness several times, though I couldn't keep count—the pain in my ribs and back was nearly all-consuming. Thoughts of my uncertain future kept creeping into my head, the terror of the unknown threatening to drown me.

I was jolted out of my pain-laced stupor when my captors stopped for a break. They produced wine, cheese, meats, and bread, then left me bound and gagged at the edge of the clearing like a forgotten piece of luggage. It had been more than twelve hours since my last meal, and I keenly felt the lack of nourishment.

"Are you hungry?" asked the man with my teeth marks tattooed on his arm.

Sensing another trap, I stared back with no

expression—there was no amount of deal-making I was willing to do for table scraps. At least not yet.

"It's your turn to carry her," the man who had, until now, been my human mule said.

"Fuck that. She bit me. Make her walk," my tormentor replied, turning back to his meal.

Thinking I would relish the chance to walk some of the stiffness out of my injuries, I waited with bated breath as my ankle cuffs were unlocked.

I couldn't have been more wrong.

With every step, my back twisted and jolted, irritating the open wound. My ribs spat fire into my lungs, causing pitiful little gasps of pain to escape my lips. It wasn't long before the slavers were pushing me roughly ahead. Before I was tripping over my feet in a bid to keep up to their long-legged strides.

"Thank fuck. I see the slavers," Mule said from beneath a dark scowl, wiping sweat from his brow when we reached the main road.

"Matthew! We were almost done waiting. I'm glad you've made it, and with the villain in tow! Wonderful, wonderful," a man wearing an expensive-looking overcoat said as he clasped hands with each of my captors.

"Our payment?" Matthew asked, his grip tightening painfully over the whip lash on my shoulder.

"Ah, yes. Here we are. As agreed upon," he said, handing over a heavy leather bag that jingled from one set of hands to the other.

Bounty hunters.

Hired thugs paid to dupe me.

I hung my head in shame.

"Now, let's have a look at our little wood menace, shall we?" the expensive man said as Matthew pushed me away. "Oh my! She certainly won't sell for very much, will she? You are a girl, yes?" he asked, removing my gag and turning my head this way and that.

My knotted brown hair decorated with braids and feathers, walnut-stained face, and tattered homespun clothing must have made quite an impression. I smirked, showing off the full wattage of a fierce, unnatural grin.

The slaver's head snapped back in surprise, and he hastily removed his hand from my face.

"Careful, them teeth ain't just for show," the bitten man said, holding up his arm.

I licked my lips.

"Feisty—gotcha," the slaver said. "We'll keep her locked down. Anything else?"

"Might need medical attention—but the bounty said dead or alive, so we figured a few scratches and bruises wouldn't make a difference," Mathew said, as he divided the cash between his companions.

With an inelegant snort, I rolled my eyes. Broken bones and lacerations were a more apt description of my current state.

"No, no, that won't matter. Auction is *take-it-or-*

leave-it. I'd imagine she'll be a good fit for the latter category. This one's headed for the salt mines," he mused. "Nothing like some honest manual labor under the lash to fix an attitude, eh? But no matter. It's worth it to have her stopped. You've done a marvelous job, gentlemen. Ladies. I'll be sure to contact you directly if I'm ever in need of your services again."

With that, the bounty hunters walked out of my life without so much as a backward glance.

I had a new threat to contend with.

"What shall we call you then, dear?" the expensive man asked as he pushed me toward a strange-looking cage containing several other captives.

His hand brushed the lash on my back and I hissed in pain, but said nothing. Seething in silence.

"No matter. We'll name you Hob. You look like a hobgoblin and smell like a dumpster, so I think it's a rather fitting moniker, hmm?"

Feet stumbling, I stopped. Gaze flicking over the majestic carriage idly hovering over the road.

The last time I'd seen it, it had been nothing more than a drawing on my father's desk. A magnetic carriage—of *Tritan* design. Intended as a solution to the energy crisis, the magnetic car used the earth's magnetic field for propulsion—a more noble project hadn't been taken on in years.

And now it was being used to transport slaves to auction.

Corrupted. Yet another Tritan treasure ruined by the empire.

I dug my nails into my palms as fury burned through my blood.

"Don't like that name?" he asked, breaking into my thoughts. Making my brain skip a beat as I tried to focus on the present. "Too bad. It suits you." With that, he gave me a vicious shove and locked the door of the magnetic carriage behind me. The terrified faces of my cellmates stared at me in what I could only imagine was revulsion.

A trembling hand reached out, making me cringe. I focused on the savagely beaten profile of a girl no older than me. A girl who, even beneath the greenish tint of bruised skin, was beautiful. Her highlighted brown hair and sparkling green eyes a magnet I couldn't look away from when she asked, "You're the one who was freeing Elorans?"

I nodded once.

"You got the rest of my family to safety. They sent me word from across the sea before I tried to flee. Thank you, a thousand times, thank you!" she said, eyes shimmering with tears. "My name's Kyra. What's yours?"

Baffled, I could only stare.

Thankfully, the slaver chose that moment to start the car, and the unique experience of hovering above the ground distracted Kyra from her pursuit of friendship.

I imagined the trip was uneventful for the other girls, who clutched at each other for support, while I stared at the passing buildings in awe. I'd lost track of how many years I'd spent in the woods, and seeing a flourishing civilization for the first time since my exile was completely overwhelming. The sheer volume of people going about their business made my heart beat erratically and sweat bead on my brow. The smells a suffocating nightmare I couldn't escape. Not even with my eyes shut, trying to place myself in the sanctity of my forest.

Sucking a breath through my teeth, I tried not to hear the sounds of a thriving city. Tried instead to view my surroundings with a rational mind as I searched for an escape.

The buildings were mostly intact, absent the war scars I'd been expecting to see, given the stories I'd heard from escaped slaves and refugees.

No one looked twice at a slave transport.

It took us the better part of the afternoon to enter the city proper, and I'd spent most of that time pressed against the bars farthest from my fellow captives. Serenaded by terrified sobs of my fellow prisoners, each choked whimper growing more and more heart-wrenching as we neared our destination. I could understand their fear—better yet, I shared it —no one valued freedom more than I did.

But I let their terror ground me, separate and distant. Let it give me the benefit of a clear perspective as I spent hours searching for a chance to make a break for it. During this passive observation of my surroundings, it was the strong military presence that stuck out the most.

We were headed toward a war zone, which could only mean one thing—elites.

Being worked to death in the salt mines would be a blessing.

The carriage slid to a graceful halt before a building of red, crumbling brick.

"Jasper! Good to see you, mate. Slaves for the front line?" a soldier asked as he came forward to meet the carriage.

"Indeed, Kyle, and a sorry lot they are, I might add. Except for this one," he replied, stroking Kyra's hair through the bars. "A little rough around the edges, but I'd imagine she's the only one of worth." He sighed, and Kyle laughed.

I glared at him through the bars. Reckless. Angry.

"Good *Lord*, where did you find *that* one?" Kyle asked, dark eyebrows jumping to meet his hairline as he caught my gaze. The revulsion billowed off him in waves.

A satisfied smile traced my lips, injected with every ounce of hate I could muster.

"Ah, yes. This unfortunate creature is Hob. She's the wood menace who's been poisoning my men and freeing slaves. Say hello, Hob," Jasper said, jabbing me painfully in the ribs.

I bared my teeth, and Kyle clapped, amused.

"She's a right wild little thing, isn't she? Oy! Caleb! Come see this," Kyle shouted, waving over another soldier. Soon enough, there was a crowd of men gathering around our cage, pointing and laughing. I did my best to remain impassive, but with Jasper stabbing his stick at me, it was all I could do not to shriek in rage.

"All right, all right, that's enough," Jasper said, laughing along with the soldiers. "If you want to see her, come to the auction tonight. Nine o'clock sharp!"

I curled in on myself as we started moving again, fists rolled into white-knuckled balls. Vision going blurry as terrified sobs threatened to overwhelm me.

A gentle hand settled on my shoulder.

"I'm sorry," Kyra said in a soft voice. She pressed closer, wriggling into my side, then draped her arm around my shoulders.

Her touch was a comfort that bolstered my courage, so I indulged in the contact. But only for a moment. My tolerance worn thin and ragged, I pulled away, but pressed a trembling hand to my heart in thanks.

By the time we'd come to a stop behind a battered building, I'd managed to pull myself together. Here were the war scars I'd been looking for. Most of the windows were either broken or boarded up, the walls blackened by fire. Yet, the sounds of merriment spilled from inside, hinting at a gathering of a great many people.

One by one, the other girls were dragged from the transport cage, leaving me alone behind bars.

Caged.

Biding my time.

Left to my own devices, I tried everything I could think of—pulled on the cage's floorboards and tried to squeeze between the tight spaces between the bars. Pacing and sweating, one arm a tight, supportive band around my ribs. Fingers sticky with dried blood.

There was nothing for it.

I'd have to fight my way past Jasper when he returned or accept my fate in the salt mines. But there was only one way out of this cage.

When the sounds coming from the building swelled, I stilled. Muscles tense. Coiled for the strike.

Jasper's eyes were bright with excitement—until he looked at me. Taking in my defensive posture, he slowed his approach and collected a set of handcuffs. With a deliberately slow twist of his wrist, he unlocked the cage and stepped inside.

Panic rushed through my system, and I lashed out, dragging my nails down the side of his face. I hadn't the leverage to draw blood, but there were now angry red slashes running the length of his face.

Absent any hint of mirth, Jasper laughed. And it was cruel. "I thought so, Hob," he mused, seizing my wrists in a bruising grip. Overpowered and overwhelmed in seconds. And before I could defend myself, I was bound in heavy iron manacles, a thick matching collar snapped shut about my throat. Pinching where the hinge nipped at my skin.

And though I had yet to utter a word, the temptation to curse and scream until I was blue in the face nearly overwhelmed me. The final insult occurred as he snapped the end of his walking stick to the loop at the front of my collar and dragged me from the cage.

The heavy chains connecting my wrists threw me off balance and I stumbled, nearly garroting myself on the collar.

"Easy, Hob," he said in a tone reserved for soothing unruly children or wild animals.

I exploded in anger, a wordless scream escaping my lips as I lunged at him, intent on ending his life. He stepped out of range, keeping me at the end of the stick as I clawed at the collar, drawing blood. It was disturbingly easy for him to lead me through the door the other captives had gone through, using the stick as leverage.

And so, my introduction to the auction house was at the end of a pole I'd only seen a dog catcher use. Cheeks flushed in fury.

Jasper drove me forward, tight in my shadow until I was off-center on a small stage. Staring stupidly back at the hundreds of soldiers crammed into the small room.

The other women were arranged on the stage to

my left, unrestrained. All but Kyra—who was directly beside me—were shaking with fear, tears streaking down their faces. Her beautiful pale face was covered in healing bruises, yet she retained an air of haughty purity.

"Can't wait to wipe that look off her face," one man shouted, reaching to grab at his crotch. Leering. His pupils wide, nostrils pinched white.

Unbroken, beautiful Kyra was drawing too much attention.

Lips parting, I was suddenly desperate to warn her of her mistake.

But the damage was done.

Picking out entire conversations in the roar of the crowd was next to impossible, but comments about beautiful green eyes were clear enough.

A commotion from the crowd drew my attention away from my fellow captives. Several serving girls brought drinks and food around. Girls who seemed to be on the menu *themselves*, for as I watched, horrified, the poor creatures offered strained smiles at the men who groped them at will —high, brittle laughter for those who grew bold enough to drag them over a lap. Touching and tasting, some going so far as to fight over the prettiest ones.

Teeth bared, I reached without thinking. Fingers seeking Kyra and the soft comfort her touch might offer.

Jasper jerked the stick, and I was forced to my knees with an anguished cry.

"Shall we start the bidding?" Jasper cried after passing my lead to one of his men. "This first Eloran treasure has the perfect temperament for a novice trainer..." said Jasper as he pulled the terrified girl to the forefront.

But I could no longer hear him, his voice drowned out as I tried to quell the terror screaming inside my head. Watching as he proceeded down the line, selling girl after girl, relentless until the woman standing next to Kyra sold for eight thousand dollars.

When the stage was cleared of everyone else, Jasper clapped his hands together and shouted over the din. "Gentlemen, this is our main event of the evening!" The crowd fell silent, watching as Jasper hauled me to my feet. "May I introduce Hob. This horrible little creature has been living in the forest for some time, poisoning my men and freeing slaves. But this delicate Eloran rose," he said, stroking Kyra's face tenderly. "Has befriended her. And yes, there is a female under all this filth," he said, and they erupted into laughter.

Teeth clenched, I let my glare fall to the floorboard beneath my boots. I never thought I'd be bothered by the opinion of others, but when tears pooled in my eyes at the merciless taunting, I knew I'd been wrong.

Kyra's fingers slipped into my clenched fist, and

she squeezed, sending me the support she could.

"This beautiful girl stubbornly refuses to see Hob's hideous exterior and seeks to comfort the little beast!" he exclaimed, lifting our joined hands in triumph.

The applause was deafening—men laughing and placing bets. Lewd comments echoed and blended together as a wash of numb fell over my mind. Horror drenching me in a cold sweat.

Jasper spread his fingers, then caught Kyra's chin between forefinger and thumb. "Kyra's charms are matched only by her stubborn will, gentlemen, so she is suitable only for those with experience. Wouldn't want to damage such a treasure, would we? Shall we start the bidding at ten thousand?"

Kyra's eyes widened in surprise.

And then her cheeks went pale, translucent, as the bidding became fierce beyond anything I'd ever seen.

But when a giant of a man stood and shouted, "Twenty-five thousand!" the tears began to fall. Her proud face streaked with anguish seemed only to ignite the men, and when the other bidders were silent for the count of ten, Jasper announced her sale. Rings flashing as he twisted his fingers, positively alight with glee.

I moved to give her the small comfort she'd given me moments before, but I was jerked back by the man holding my lead.

Gone. Led off the stage with only a single, fragile backward glance. A brittle smile meant to comfort me as her new owner collected her in massive arms.

It took a few minutes, but the crowd eventually settled enough for Jasper to make his next pitch.

Mine.

"For those of you who enjoy a challenge, this is your girl," he said, palming the back of my neck. Sneering, he glared into my face. "She certainly doesn't seem like much. Honestly, I should be paying you to take her off my hands, but Hob comes with a nasty little bag of tricks!" He gave the collar a vicious tug, making me gasp in surprise and bare my teeth.

The crowd cheered.

"You couldn't pay me to stick my dick in that mouth, Jasper!" called a man from the front. "Seems too risky for such important equipment."

"She'd be doing us all a favor, stopping you from reproducing," the man to his left shouted, and the crowd erupted into laughter again.

"Shall we start the bidding at one hundred dollars?" Jasper asked, and the crowd was suddenly a mix of laughter and astonishment.

I hadn't been a part of society for some time, but even I knew that was an outrageously low price for a slave. I lost the battle with my pride as my head bowed under the pressure of the cruelty these people heaped on me.

"I'll give you fifty," came a lazy drawl from the

center of the crowd.

The room went silent, except for the sound of my grinding teeth.

Throat aching, my breath caught. Blinking until my vision cleared, I lifted my gaze, unable to resist the temptation to see the face of the man who had made the offer. Who would dare to assign so little worth to a life?

For a moment, there was nothing. Silence as I scanned the crowd, glaring through a wave of humiliated tears.

My eyes landed on an inky, unblinking stare framed by a lazy smile.

Lips parted, I froze.

My priestess gifts, which until now had been easily subdued, flared to life.

Ravenous, pulsing energy swirled just out of sight. Seething with the sort of power I'd never known, it spat dark flames at the edges of my senses. Reached for me with greedy fingers dipped in pitch.

And I knew, without a doubt, I was looking into the eyes of a tightly coiled predator.

A Caledonian elite.

Rational thought fled, and I pulled back on the stick so sharply Jasper lost his balance. The crowd exploded into laughter as two burly men wrestled me into a kneeling position and chained me to the floor.

"Sold!" Jasper cried, sending me a hate-filled glare.

5

"Aww, Captain, what the hell?" asked a man to the left of the elite as the crowd began to disperse. "She's awful! Dirty and—"

"We lost ground today, Marco. Tell me," the elite drawled, adjusting his sleeve without breaking eye contact with me, "why should I reward you lot of ingrates with a good quality slave?"

"But that green-eyed one was *so* pretty, and you didn't even make an offer."

Without another word, the captain rose from his seat and approached the stage. His gait smooth, absent any hint of hesitation.

Trying to determine if he could feel me the same way I could feel him, I held eye contact, fighting not to blink in the face of all that power. The raw, explosive energy searching for an outlet.

An *elite.*

Not just here, but my new owner.

My eyes flicked to the edge of the state, catching for an instant on a battered door before snapping back to the predator dressed in a man's flesh.

Claiming a key ring from Jasper, he knelt and said, "What's your name, little slave?" Voice a soothing hum that only wound me tighter.

Still, hardly daring to breathe, I waited until he'd finished unlocking my chains and cuffs, then burst into action. Heart hammering with desperate energy, I came to life despite the fire crackling between my ribs. I tried to dash away—only to be caught and pinned by strong arms.

"Not so fast, pet."

I choked on a scream, clawing and scratching at any exposed skin I could reach. Struggling until his arms tightened. Until something popped. Something *inside* that felt like an icicle shattering on the coldest winter day. Brittle. *Fragile.* The pain so intense, breath froze in my lungs. Limbs held stiff as sweat bloomed across my nape, stinging where it seeped into the lash mark. Any lingering fight extinguished in an instant, I went rigid.

To his credit, the captain eased off as soon as my demeanor changed, though I was already shaking. And against my ear, "I asked you a question."

"She hasn't spoken yet, sir," Jasper said with a helpful shrug. "Perhaps she's simple."

"Ah." The captain turned, bringing me with him

to face the slaver. "So, not only were your men outsmarted by a girl, but she was also an incapable one. Do I understand you correctly?"

Jasper offered a greasy bow. An elegant little flourish. "A point well made, sir. May I ask what you're planning for her?"

Nose wrinkled, the captain pushed me back, inspecting me with a narrow glare and wrinkled nose. "First order of business is a bath. I'd like to see what's under all this filth."

"And then?" Jasper prompted, eying me maliciously.

"Easy, slaver. I can't tell if I have a diamond or a lump of coal just yet. Why the interest?" the captain asked, propelling me toward a door.

"She's caused me a lot of trouble over the years, and now *this*," Jasper said, gesturing to the scratches on his face. "I owe her a debt."

A tremor raced through my muscles as the sweat dripped and dripped. Pain and fear competing for the right to make me shiver.

The captain frowned. "Why not settle this so-called debt before the auction?"

"Bad form to sell used slaves! Well," Jasper chuckled, "that, and I had a deadline to keep. Debts of a different nature to settle."

The captain hummed, herding me through the door I'd meant to use as an escape.

Stumbling, nauseous and cold, my mind began to

skip. Wandering, only peripherally listening to the conversation flowing around me as I looked for a means of escape.

"If she's a suitable pleasure slave, I'll let you know. She might be more profitable in the fighting rings, so no guarantees," the captain said, directing my path. "Though, if my men continue to perform like they did today, I'll make her the only pleasure slave they have access to."

"It was a bad day, Captain Rawlings. Have a heart," Marco cried, clutching his chest. "What do you think it will do for company morale if she's—"

"I will personally ensure you never use another pleasure slave, soldier," the captain snapped, voice tight with warning. "Pleasure slaves are a reward for your efficiency in combat, not something you're entitled to. And because I pay for them and train them, I can also prevent your access to them. Don't fuck with me today, Marco."

I chanced a glance at Marco and found him flushed, cheeks pink beneath a ruddy tan. Captain Rawlings, the elite, must be a force to be reckoned with.

And he was my new owner.

Sucking air between clenched teeth, I took shallow breaths as I was driven through the streets at a clipped pace. But with every step I was forced to take, my ribs jolted and bumped. My vision blurred around the edges, ears ringing a high-pitched whine.

And then my head began to tilt—heavy on the left, my ears filled with bubbles as my lips tingled. Face going numb.

A bathhouse swam into my line of sight, but I was barely keeping pace. Halfway to senseless when the captain pushed the door open.

Squealing laughter and perfume assaulted my already-reeling senses. My breath fogged with the sticky heat of a public bath, and I stumbled. Gagging on humid air, my palms struck the hard concrete.

Hauled up by the back of my rough-spun shirt before I had a chance to react, I was set on my feet as strong fingers dug into the whip lashes, opening the wound where the flesh hadn't even begun to mend.

All I could offer was a grimace. A slight inhale that whistled at the back of my throat.

Releasing me with a curse, the captain pulled back. Palm soaked red and sticky. "Shit. Are you injured, slave?" he asked, and with clean knuckles, caught the edge of my jaw. Turning my face toward him.

A snort of laughter bubbled up, escaping through my nose. The cold had spilled all the way down my back, leaving me numb. Swaying, palms tingling, the world tilted back and everything went white.

6

———————

I awoke without opening my eyes.

Wrapped in strong arms, rocking side to side.

I was being carried.

Making sure there was nothing wrong with any of my limbs, I took a mental inventory of my body. The instant I was sure I was capable, I came to life, struggling until I was dropped with a curse. Ribs screamed a desperate protest, but I knew.

This was my second wind. My last chance to make a break for it.

Blind to the pain, I started running as soon as I had my feet under me.

Despite the size of the bathhouse, it was all but empty. A blessing and a hindrance, for while there were few to aid in my recapture, neither could I lose myself in a crowd.

My only hope lay in my superior agility from all my years running in the trees. In the unique set of skills I'd fought so hard to claim.

On my right, a spiral staircase sloping gently to the second floor caught my eye, and I veered off without warning. The sensation of narrowly escaping capture made my heart flutter, and I poured everything I had into my mad dash.

Heavy feet thundered behind me, closing the narrow gap.

I jumped, trusting my instincts, my eyes fixed to the wide banister.

"Sonofa—" Hooked fingers slipped off the back of my shirt.

With a squeal, I looked and saw the blur of a Caledonian man. Taking the stairs three at a time, he paced me easily.

I grinned. The banister was polished wood, but it wasn't much different from running on branches slick with freezing rain. Easier by far than trying to do it silently.

There was shouting coming from all around me now. Barked orders from the stairs on my left, answered from those still on the floor below.

But I could hear nothing over the sound of my own pounding heart. My ragged, wet breaths that spoke of internal harm I couldn't just walk off.

When I reached the second floor, I launched myself from the railing. Sailing through the air, I landed with a thump that awoke the pain in my ribs from the dull roar it had become. A splinter of breathtaking agony, muted, no doubt, by the adrenaline coursing through my veins.

A large man wearing nothing but a towel appeared in front of me, thick thighs blocking my path.

I skidded to a halt, sides heaving painfully. And when our eyes met, I recoiled—this man was an elite warrior and far more powerful than Captain Rawlings. His energy tainted with a scent I recognized in an instant.

And then I knew two things at once. *This* elite had an enslaved priestess feeding him energy, and Captain Rawlings did not.

The consequences of being caught by either man were opposite ends of the same horrible stick.

Eyes wild, I searched for another exit.

"Nowhere to go, Hob," the captain drawled from behind me, spurring me into startled action.

Surprising even myself, I rushed the elite in front of me, then dove between his spread legs, yanking the towel from his hips as I went.

But instead of moving to cover himself, the big man merely laughed. Rumbling deep and cruel, absent any shred of humility. "You've got a wild one, Asher," he said in a deep, throaty voice I could feel in my chest.

Light shone through a window at the end of the hall, beckoning. The outlet I needed, and my very last chance. I lengthened my steps, trying to make it before the elites could get their hands on me.

At full speed, I slammed into the wall, clawing at the windowsill, trying to pry it open.

But it didn't budge.

And then, "It's sealed shut, Hob," the captain said, voice a steady, soothing drum.

A strangled cry burst from my throat. "No!" My voice was distorted with disuse, I sobbed. Terrified, refusing to give up. My fists met the glass in a flurry of desperation, trying to break it.

Utterly hopeless, a waste of energy I couldn't spare, I was a wild thing caught behind glass. Betrayed by instinct that had demanded I seek the highest ground, I was left with nothing but to face my captors.

Spinning, fists clenched, I scowled through the blur of tears.

"Easy, Hob," the captain cooed, advancing on me. "That's it. Easy."

Tears spilled over my lashes, and I adopted a fighting stance. Legs trembling with exhaustion.

He had the nerve to laugh.

I sucked an outraged breath between my teeth, ignoring the barb of hurt—the humiliation.

"Would you get a look at that!" the naked elite

said as Marco joined us in the narrow hall, crowding me in. "She looks like an angry little wildcat."

Breathless, Marco said, "The rest of the slaves are out of the building."

Nodding, the captain took another tentative step. "Make this easy on yourself," he said. Reasonable and calm.

I sneered.

Faster than I thought possible, he lunged. One hand finding an anchor in my hair, the other winding tight about my throat. The crook of his elbow pinching beneath my chin with bruising strength, adding pressure with nothing but a flex of his bicep.

And I was left struggling in his arms, fighting as hard as I could until my whole body shook with exertion and sweat coated my skin once more.

The captain wasn't even winded when he pressed his lips to my ear and snarled, "Enough."

I clawed at his tanned skin, trying to draw blood.

Adding pressure to the back of my head, he cut off my air. Squeezing until my head spun and black stars danced at the edges of my vision.

Until I stopped, yielding at last.

"General Tilcot, would you mind putting on some clothes?" the captain drawled, and turned. His chest to my back, he walked me out of the narrow hall. Giving no quarter.

General Tilcot rushed ahead. "Don't start without me, Captain. I want to see what our wildcat looks like under all *this*." He plucked at my clothes with a grimace.

Dragging me back down the stairs, the captain stopped in front of a large pool of water with waist-high stone walls. Silent until Marco retrieved a matronly woman from another room.

With a single glance, she tsked her disapproval. "And just what am I to do with this mess, sir?" she said in a shrill voice.

Gathering my wrists, Captain Rawlings said, "Beau, this is Hob. My newest acquisition. Haven't decided what I want to do with her just yet."

And then he lifted my hands above my head and fastened them to chains hanging from the ceiling.

Left with no way to favor my injuries, stretched taut, I cried out in pain. Stiff without the benefit of adrenaline as a painkiller.

The captain shushed me and drew a wicked-looking blade. Careless and cruel.

Through the tears streaking down my cheeks, I glared. Silent when he turned that knife on my treasured clothing with little ceremony, not stopping until there was a crumpled heap on the floor and I was naked before an audience.

Beau gasped when my torso was exposed.

"Fucking slavers!" Captain Rawlings hissed, and tossed his blade onto a nearby table.

Marco cleared his throat. "Overheard Jasper saying he hired bounty hunters to catch her. Must have caused a lot of trouble." Moving from my line of sight, the soldier prodded the open wound with a delicate touch that made me hiss, but that was it. All the energy I could spare, for General Tilcot was drawing near.

I felt his approach before I could see him, such was his power.

"Would you like my Sasha to heal our little wild-cat?" the general asked after a moment of silent inspection. "There's no sense in training an injured slave."

"Sasha's services would be greatly appreciated, General, my thanks," Captain Rawlings replied.

If there were any hint of color left in my dirty face, it drained at the mention of Sasha. I was *right*. Tilcot was bound to a priestess. The *High* Priestess, who'd been in charge of the temple before Tritan fell.

Our most powerful healer and the one to test prospective young priestess, Sasha was the one woman my father had worked so hard to hide me from. A woman who'd be able to feel my modest power the instant she laid eyes on me—*who was bound to a Caledonian general.*

Helpless but to brace for whatever came next, I let go a held breath, sagging into my restraints.

"Come to the bathhouse, Sasha," General Tilcot ordered, speaking into a wide wrist cuff. Masculine, despite the gold and precious gems.

A few minutes later, a side door opened, revealing the very last face I wanted to see.

Sasha was the embodiment of pure Tritan elegance. Her nearly white hair hung to her slim waist, and her skin was so pale it might be mistaken for translucent. Unblemished and glowing with health. She wore a simple blue wrap that hung off her slender frame, enhancing her slight curves. Golden cuffs circled her wrists and throat—a match to the one on the general's wrist.

When crystalline blue eyes met mine, the older woman blanched a sickly shade of green.

She knew.

"She's thin for a pleasure slave," Marco said from behind me. "I like it when there's something to hold on to, you know? A woman is supposed to have curves. A man has muscles." He grabbed my hips, testing his grip. Fingers kneading.

Lip curled, Captain Rawlings rolled his eyes. "Don't you have something to do, soldier?"

"Not a thing more interesting than this," Marco replied.

"Sasha, don't just stand there staring, you foolish girl! Get your ass over here," General Tilcot growled.

It was enough to make her jump, to see her rush to his side like the obedient little slave she was.

I hung my head, waiting for her to give me away.

"What's her story, my lord?" Sasha asked, and my

eyes filled with tears at the sound of her voice—it had been years since I'd heard a Tritan accent.

"Not sure. She doesn't say much. She's Captain Rawlings' newest purchase, and it seems the slavers have treated her badly," the general said, stroking Sasha's hair affectionately.

As I watched the display, my stomach flipped, revolted by the affection so obvious between slave and master.

"See what you can do for her, pet. I'm sure the captain would like to get to her training."

With that, Sasha approached. Slow, palms up, she offered a smile when all I could do was glare. And when cold hands touched the bruised skin on my ribs, I cringed, chains tinkling above my head.

"It's okay," she murmured. "I'm not going to hurt you. I'm going to take away the pain."

I felt it then—the pure energy of a healer flowing into my body. The rush of my gift as it flooded to the surface, drawn into her power. Instinctively trying to lend her strength.

Fingers dug into my skin—a warning. "Try to relax," she said, voice tight.

I understood what wasn't said. That this needed to be a routine healing, unremarkable in every way, or I risked discovery. Not bold enough to question her loyalty, I forced my power back through sheer force of will.

By the time she had finished, sweat was pouring

down my face. The pain was all but gone, and I took a deep breath, luxuriating in my ability to do so.

"What's wrong with her?" the captain asked, peering into my eyes.

"She's terrified, sir," Sasha said. "But she should be fine after some rest."

Surprise flickered across his face. "You can feel that?"

Sasha patted my knee, avoiding my eye. "Yes, sir. She's making me jittery."

Slinging a possessive arm about her shoulders, the general pulled her to his side and said, "I'd like to know what happens to this slave, Asher." He turned, preparing to leave. "She's made my morning very entertaining."

Agreeing to bring me along to lunch, they exchanged their goodbyes. Sasha threw me an encouraging look over her shoulder as they departed, and all I could do was swallow a homesick sob.

"Time for a bath, sir?" Beau asked.

"Yes, and I think we'll keep her restrained for now," the captain said. His hand settled on my lower back, and he guided me into the warm water of the bathing pool.

I gasped as my body was submerged, shocked by the luxury of warm water. Eyes sliding shut on a quiet groan. Having spent years washing with melted snow and cold river water, this was a glorious change of pace.

"Feels good, doesn't it, slave?"

Eyes snapping open, I stiffened, snapping out of my momentary lapse in guarded control.

Leaning against the edge of the pool with an amused smirk tracing his lips, the captain said, "This is called *bathing*." He said it slowly, flicking his fingers first to me, then the hot water. "You'll be doing this regularly now."

My cheeks grew hot. Scowling, I shifted in my chains to hide the hurt, the lash of humiliation.

Putting a rough brush to my freshly healed back, Beau went to work, scrubbing vigorously.

I tried to pull away, to protect myself from this indignity, but there was nowhere to go. Nothing I could do to stop them from looking at me with the same interest one might show a rabid animal.

Rolling his sleeves back, revealing corded forearms, the captain produced a bucket. Dunked it in the water swirling around my hips, then dumped it over my head.

I spluttered, choking on a cough. Eyes burning, I tried to blink away the sting. Rubbing my face on the inside of my arms, but I found no relief.

A low whistle made me flinch, and I blinked through tears to find Marco appraising me with raised brows. "Look at the state of that water, and she's *still* filthy," he said. "Captain, I promise to do double duty next week. Please don't make her a pleasure slave. *Please*. The fighters like being dirty. She'd fit right in—"

"And last about thirty seconds before I'd have a broken slave to deal with. Go do something else, Marco. You're distracting me," the captain drawled, and poured another bucket over my head.

Finished scrubbing my back, Beau squirted some pink, fruity-smelling soap into her hand and moved onto massaging my scalp.

"I may need the other girls in here, sir. And some scissors," Beau said, tugging at a particularly thick clump of hair. "Are these *feathers*?"

I squirmed when her fingers caught and wouldn't budge. My entire scalp moved as she tried to yank it free.

"Try your best to brush it out," the captain replied, then barked, "Head back," before dumping another bucket over me.

With just enough time to obey, I blinked as dark, soapy water flooded back. Running down my chest, swirling around my thighs.

A new wave of burning dripped into my eyes, and I squeezed them shut, letting the tears fall where none might see my shame.

"Beau?" the captain asked, tugging on a tuft of pubic hair covering the core of my femininity—also dyed a rich, dark brown. "Get some wax."

And then my breath caught.

The dye.

In the panic of the last few hours, of being captured, beaten, and sold, I'd forgotten. Burning eyes reminded me just how short the lifespan of homemade walnut dye might be.

Mixed with shampoo? There was no telling how soon my lineage would be revealed.

Only that it *would*.

7

When at last the women were finished with their undertaking, my skin glowed pink and was completely unblemished by walnut stains. My hair had been brushed straight, shortened by several inches, and in some places stripped bare. Smooth.

Worse, it was now a soft, flowing caramel that drew the other women in. Fawning over something that had anxiety bubbling up the back of my throat.

One more wash, *maybe* two, and the last of my disguise would melt away.

It had taken *hours* to turn me into a frilly doll dressed in thin scraps of silk.

Every humiliating moment overseen by the watchful, inky glare of one Captain Asher Rawlings.

"Well, would you look at that," Marco said, watching Beau lead me from the bathing area. "The wildcat's been transformed into a real girl," he said, reaching out to touch me.

I bared my teeth in warning.

"But perhaps not quite civilized," the captain said, a heavy hand landing on my shoulder.

Flinching, I tried to pull away.

His grip tightened, and it was enough to quell another rebellion. "What will I call you?" he asked. "Hob is a terrible name for a pleasure slave."

Instead of answering, I scowled, letting him see the seething rage bubbling just beneath the surface.

With an indignant shriek, Beau spun on her heel and slapped me with an open hand.

My head snapped to the side, but I was too shocked to make a sound.

"Of all the insolent, ungrateful—"

I didn't give her time to finish her sentence. Lunging, fueled by rage, I shirked the captain's hold too fast for him to react. My fist connected with her face so hard I was sure I'd broken something, but I continued attacking, wrapping my hands around her throat. Squeezing with the intent to crush that delicate cartilage.

A thick bicep circled my throat, ending the short-lived retaliation that had me clawing at his forearm once more. "Stop," the captain snarled, lips moving against my ear. The hard length of a muscular body dwarfed me in an unforgiving cage.

A body trained for war.

His anger a cold lash against my skin, an assault to my untrained senses, it was a dare for me to fight. The promise of retribution.

I was outmatched, my slight stature best suited for stealth attacks, for subterfuge and poison. Not *this*. Not hand-to-hand combat against an opponent more than twice my size.

Lifting trembling hands, I surrendered.

A smile flicked against my skin, pressed into my perfectly groomed hair. "Good girl," he murmured, and let me breathe but kept me pressed to his chest. Restrained.

"How dare you?" Beau hissed, clutching a swollen cheek as she glared through tears. Body stiff as Marco helped her to stand.

"Beau." The captain's voice was sharp with warning. A clear reprimand.

I met her watery glare, a taunting smile tracing my lips.

"Punish her!" she screamed, then froze. Her skin blanched a sickly shade of green. "Sir," she added in a terrified squeak, her eyes rimmed in white.

"Hob's training is no concern of yours," the captain replied, cold. Clipped.

"I'm sorry, sir," she whispered, head bowed. "I have no idea what's come over me."

I sneered, a tiny puff of disgusted air crossing my lips as I took a step away from her.

A fist wrapped in my hair, and the captain forced

my neck to arch. My head made to rest against his shoulder. "Something funny?"

My lips parted, but nothing came out.

"You're forgiven, of course, Beau," he said, voice rumbling against my back. "Take the rest of the day for yourself, and get that eye looked at."

"Thank you," she whispered, and fled the room.

Marco grinned. "Quite the right cross you've got there, wildcat."

"Get out," the captain snapped in an icy tone.

"Yes, sir," the soldier replied with a salute before he too disappeared.

When we were alone, the captain sighed. A casual thing laced with simmering violence I could taste, that forced a high-pitched whine through my lips. "It's time you learned your place, pet," he said, and with a calm brutality, twisted my right arm behind my back.

He marched me through the exit into the brisk air, not letting up on my arm until we'd entered the remains of a beautiful old townhouse.

The sight made my heart ache. My parents had owned a similar residence before the war, and I'd spent many nights curled up in a comfortable chair as I listened to my father regale us with tales of Tritan politics as we sipped tea with biscuits.

In a blur, he forced me through the front door, down the hall, and past the kitchen without slowing. He didn't stop until I was trembling in the middle of a comfortable study. The door slammed shut with a sharp snap.

"Beau has been in my family for thirty years," he said, looming over me. "Not once in that entire time has she lost her temper, nor has a single person raised a hand to her, so what," he drawled, "is it about *you* that evokes such passion, hmm?"

Swallowing a thick lump of terror, I shrugged. Affecting an air of insolence, I knew I was playing with fire, but I was too tired and angry to care.

His gaze darkened, glare burning into mine as I tried my best not to blink. To remain neutral in the face of this man.

An elite.

The weight of his unwavering attention heavy enough that my legs began to shake. Fidgeting without daring to blink, caught in the inky pool of swirling, insatiable hunger where darkness festered.

"Let's start with your name, shall we?" he murmured, opening a drawer and arranging a series of cruel-looking whips and crops across the polished desktop. And then, with rolling hips, the captain stalked toward me. The embodiment of deadly grace I'd only seen once before—in the gait of a mountain lion.

I stepped back, tripping over bare feet as fear poked through my mask of careful indifference.

"I'll ask you once more," he said, and touched my chin with a curled knuckle. "And then things are going to get very unpleasant for you. What is your name?"

Silence yawned between us. My breaths shallow.

Pure, unfiltered menace rose to meet my continued disobedience. And in a grip that was almost *gentle*, he caught my wrists in one large, calloused hand. Pulled me into his chest.

It was an action that might have been considered tender if not for the trembling of our bodies—one in fear, the other in anger.

"I like doing things the hard way," he said conversationally. Quiet in the intimacy of such close quarters. Precise, calculated when he snapped a set of cuffs on my wrists and dragged me to a hook dangling from the ceiling. "It just feels good to accomplish something no one else can—or wants to, in your case."

His tone stopped me from reacting to the hurt, but it was the greedy flavor of his energy that had me frozen. Too scared to fight. Too tired to hope.

I could only watch, tracking him with my eyes alone. Breathing through thin lips when he retrieved a bar with two leather bands and strapped it between my spread ankles.

Left restricted, *exposed,* he chuckled when I grew bold enough to test these new bonds. "When I ask a question, I expect an answer," he murmured, pushing a lock of caramel hair back from my brow.

It was a reasonable request. One that made my

gut clench in dreadful recognition of the slippery slope it was. That giving him *anything* was to accept this.

His rule over me.

Warm fingers slipped beneath the scraps of silk, tugging at the ties keeping them in place.

I whined, a burst of anxiety slipping free of my lips, only to be sucked back in. No matter that he'd spent the afternoon looking at... *everything*. That he'd ordered me waxed to his specifications, watching for hours as women worked.

This was so much worse.

He let the silk fall, exposing me. Close enough that I could see it when his pupils swallowed what little color his eyes possessed, black gaze fixed to my breasts. To the nipples puckered tight in the chill.

A beacon for a predator's attention.

The silk pooled around my ankles when he turned. As if the rest of my nudity held no interest for a man of his stature.

And I squirmed, the chains tinkling above my head. Hands already going numb, I eyed the assortment of whips. Dread making my muscles lock up.

"There are several ways to train a slave," he began, soft, as if we were engaged in polite conversation. "And it takes many years of practice to find a preferred method. But most agree a single tail whip is a dangerous chore. Of course, you already know this. You felt the true bite of a whip just this morning." He stepped behind me, and I shivered as he traced a warm finger where the whip's lash had been.

Had it only been this morning? I swallowed, the click of my throat audible in the hush.

"When you've trained as many slaves as I have," he continued, "you begin to see the whip as the crude tool of an amateur." He retrieved a small white bag from a shelf, ignoring the weapons laid out before me. "However, I've found the most effective punishment to be the combination of two vastly different things. This is a bag of rice," he said, holding the open bag under my nose before dumping the contents on the floor at my feet.

He loosened the chain in the ceiling, giving my arms plenty of slack.

A frown creased my brows.

"Kneel," he hummed, and thumbed my lower lip.

I sneered, deciding against obedience.

He smiled, dark eyes glittering. Seeming to enjoy my show of defiance, he pushed the hair back from my face, tangled his fingers in my caramel-colored locks, and pulled. Adding pressure to my scalp until I struggled to keep my head up or bow under pressure.

"Kneel," he said again as if this were a game.

With my ankles bound to the bar, I had no way to ease myself into it. Thumping onto the scattered rice with a hiss of pain, I grunted. Tiny grains dug into my flesh, and no matter how much I shuffled, there was no comfortable position to be found. Struggling only made it worse. Drove the grains deeper.

Gasping, I dared to meet his eye, glaring with as much silent venom as I could muster.

"Uncomfortable, isn't it?" He lowered himself, pressing too close. Making me taste the heat of his breath.

Teeth bared as sweat beaded on my brow, I almost smiled. No longer confused by his actions—this was indeed a cruel punishment.

Rising and selecting a whip with a braided leather pommel, he said, "It's been a while since a slave of mine has needed a good whipping. Hope I haven't lost my touch."

An experimental crack of the whip made me flex in horrid anticipation.

And without giving me an instant to prepare or brace, the air whistled as he brought the whip across my back hard enough to make me yelp but not enough to lay open my skin. My back arched as I writhed against the pain, my every movement grinding grains of rice into the thin skin of my knees.

"One," he said, and the air screamed again as he brought the whip down on the exposed skin of my bottom. "Two."

I gasped through clenched teeth, determined to bear this punishment in silence. By the time he got to six, I was trembling, tears streaming down my face. The pain of each new lash compounding with those that had come before, giving me no chance to recuperate, the skin of my knees broken from constant struggling. But I was nothing if not stubborn, and I had completely focused on making it to ten, the assumption being my punishment could go no farther.

"Eleven," he drawled in a dispassionate voice, and I knew then he intended to continue until I'd lost our little power struggle or I was beaten bloody.

"Stop," I whispered, voice breaking. Worn too thin to bother hoping my accent wouldn't be noticeable at this decibel.

He ran his hands over the bruised skin on my back, bottom, and thighs, making me *burn.* "Your name?"

I shook my head, moaning in pain. In fear.

"I can keep this up as long as you'd like, pet. Up to you."

"I don't remember!" I cried, panic flooding my system. Cold steel bit into my wrists as I fought with the ferocity of a trapped animal to free myself, aware I was wasting precious energy. Helpless to do anything but.

"You are a puzzle, aren't you?" he hummed, stroking my hair back when I went still at last. Exhausted. Soaked in a cold sweat that stank of fear. "I don't believe you, of course, but I've gotten everything I needed for tonight. Now, what do I expect when I ask a question?"

"An answer," I whispered, disgusted by my weakness.

"Good girl."

With little ceremony, he unlocked my bonds. Strong hands slipped beneath my armpits, and he hauled me up. All but dragged me down a narrow set of rickety stairs, despite the way I stumbled in his wake. He delivered me to a small concrete room with no windows that smelled of cleaning products and mold.

Concrete floors and walls.

A cold-room for food storage.

Absent any hint of comfort.

With a push, I stumbled into the small room, clutching at my naked skin. Trembling for too many reasons to count.

"I do hope these sleeping quarters are to your satisfaction."

I tossed a glare over my shoulder and turned away, my entire body aching with exhaustion.

"Slave," he barked. His voice was a clap of thunder in the tiny room.

I hadn't noticed the whip wound around his waist, but I very nearly screamed when he began to uncoil it.

"Yes!" I said, palms raised, voice a dry croak.

"Yes, *what*, slave?"

Tears flooded my lash line, but I let my head fall. To hide in plain sight. "Yes, *sir*."

"Good girl," he said again, staring for a while longer.

And then, almost as an afterthought, I felt him reach out. A tendril of energy stretching toward me, trying to feel what I hid beneath the surface.

Head spinning, I went white. The blood drained from my face all at once. A terrifying thought flicked through the fog between my ears.

If the most powerful priestesses could manipulate energy the same way an elite could, would the opposite be true for the elites?

If Captain Rawlings could feel my energy, it would only be a matter of time before he realized I wasn't Eloran.

Not *just* a loose Tritan.

A priestess.

I cleared my throat to break his concentration, let my hands fall, and exposed my breasts to his evil glare. Using one vulnerability to cloak another, my modest feminine wiles used to distract. To redirect.

To my horror, I felt a sudden lessening of strength in the small room. That seething energy receding, back to its master.

He stepped over the threshold, filling it with his essence. "Do you have something to say, pet?"

"No, sir." My voice was barely audible, but a smug grin flickered across his features, nevertheless.

"So pretty," he mused, stroking a finger over my lips. Touch falling, he caught my left nipple between forefinger and thumb. Pinched until I squirmed. "You'll make a fine pleasure slave someday soon. Until then, a few hours in the hole should be just the thing for your faulty memory, hmm?"

He left me then, closing the heavy door behind him.

Plunging me into complete darkness that was somehow brighter without him to fill that small space.

Collapsing, my knees went out from under me.

It was only a matter of time before he knew—what I was, what I could do. Not long before I was made to turn against my own people. Made to hunt the refugees fleeing the empire, my modest power turned against the helpless masses.

Sinking my teeth into the meat of my thumb, I trapped a scream in my throat. Crawled to the closest wall on hands and knees and pressed my burning, wounded flesh against the concrete. Instant relief flooded through my skin, cold against hot flesh aching from my latest whipping.

I spent the night like that, curled in the fetal position. On my side in the dark. Soaking in the silence, because despite the torment the captain meant to inflict in this dank little hole, there was nothing I knew better than how to be alone.

At first, the chill of the concrete floor was a soothing balm, but as the night wore on, the shaking set in.

It started with tossing and turning. The bite of tiny, frosty fingers curled around my internal organs until I could no longer just sit and wait.

Stumbling around the room, blind in the dark and trying to keep warm, I lost all track of time. Could do little but pace until I was too tired to do even that. Until I slid to the floor and wrapped myself in a hug that didn't come nearly close enough to consolation.

When the door opened, I could hardly bother to cringe back from the light. Blinking at the soldier who'd appeared in the doorway to deliver bread and a glass of water.

"Eat," the soldier barked, and when I remained pressed against the wall, he kicked the plate in my direction. "Don't make me ask twice, slave."

But despite my pacing, I'd been sitting too long. My limbs had gone stiff and tingly where they were wrapped around my knees, muscles locked in place. Nudity hidden, too cold to muster the effort to put food to mouth.

Hands balled into fists, he advanced on me, the intent to do harm written clearly on his face.

To make me obey.

Lurching into action, I scrambled for the small loaf of bread that had rolled from the plate. Stuffing my mouth full of the stale, flavorless stuff of army rations, I cringed back from him at last, trying to appease. The loaf was so dry I couldn't swallow without taking a mouthful of water to choke it down. And by the time I was halfway through, my jaw was aching, but the activity had warmed me.

Seizing my arm, the soldier waited only long enough for me to finish before he dragged me from the dark.

One arm wrapped around my breasts, I staggered along in his wake, trying to free myself from that iron grip. Fighting until we got to the front hall, and I realized we were far from alone.

Soldiers.

A score of heavily armed men milled about in the cramped quarters of the captain's home. Laughing and pushing, a cloud of cigarette smoke hung thick over their heads while others ate simple breakfasts. The dull roar of conversation oppressive—until, as one, they took notice of the naked girl shivering in their midst.

A deadly silence settled over the room before the men erupted in laughter and started cheering. Forcing me to press close to my escort, to cling to his crisp uniform. Terrified to be left without some form of protection as they drew near.

"Holy shit, Cal! Is this the wild thing from last

night's auction?" a burly soldier asked, touching my shoulder.

I jerked away from him, fingers winding tighter into Cal's coat as I was inspected. Terror surging in my blood, I trembled, eyes flicking from one leering face to the next.

"Yeah," Cal said, and dropped a steadying hand on my shoulder. "Captain got her cleaned up last night. Rawlings said she attacked Beau, so I wouldn't get too close if I were you."

Squirming, I shook my head—Beau had struck me first. I'd only defended myself.

"Shit. She's actually kind of pretty," the burly soldier said, offering a warm smile framed by chocolate eyes. "Now that I can see what's under the grime."

With a short bark of cold laughter, Cal turned me to face the crowd. Letting them look, he looped one heavy forearm around my ribs, pulled my hands away from my breasts, and dragged me back until I hissed. Showing teeth. His uniform agitating skin the captain had made tender. "Don't worry, Gabe. Rawlings'll put the fight out of her in no time, and this little thing will be free for the taking."

"Shit, I hope not! I like a little spirit now and then," Gabe said, touching my face. Not put off by my curled lip, but neither did his gaze drop to my exposed nipples. "What's your name, pretty girl?"

My only response was the most acidic glare I

could muster.

Gabe laughed, face lit with interest. Easygoing with a sparkling smile.

"He asked you a question, slave!" Cal barked, giving me a violent shake, forcing me to my bruised and bloodied knees. And then, catching a fist full of my hair, he twisted. Forcing my head back, he set my cheek to the inseam of his trousers.

Straining away from something hard that twitched against my skin, I whined. Shoulders bunched, braced for a blow—until I felt it.

Dark flames lapped at the back of my neck. The explosive energy of a predator, coiled for the strike, drawing nearer with every passing instant.

"Easy," Gabe cautioned. "You know the captain doesn't like it when you fuck with a slave he's training. Confuses the message."

"Nonsense, Gabe." Spoken in an easy drawl, it was the voice of a man who had all the time in the world.

I couldn't help it—I jumped at the sound of that smooth, cultured purr, then went utterly still. Eyes fixed to the tips of his scuffed boots when they stopped before me, I exhaled a careful stream of anxiety as the entire company stood and saluted.

Leaving me curled around myself at the captain's feet, Cal stepped back. His fingers sliding free of my hair.

"I believe you were asked a question," the captain

cooed, and when the company fell silent, he took a knee. Forearm braced atop his thigh, free hand skating up my bicep. "And here I thought we'd already gone over this." Gentle fingers caught my chin, turning my face toward him.

At the sight of his regrettably handsome face, I sucked a breath between my lips. Chills spilling down my spine as the reality of my position settled in.

Naked in a room full of soldiers. Men who looked and saw nothing more than a future pleasure slave.

Helpless. At the mercy of this one man, I swallowed, *hard*, and in an intentionally hoarse whisper said, "I don't know my name, sir." Attempting to affect an air of obedience. To avoid a punishment I might never recover from.

"Ah, yes. My little blank slate," the captain hummed, and, as I watched, a shadow traced the edge of his smirk.

One that reached his eyes in a blink.

Ensnared in an inky, bottomless void, I was held in thrall. Sucked deeper the longer I looked.

And despite how I wanted to twist away, I *couldn't*, even when his thumb moved to trace the bow of my lower lip. When it caught and pulled, exposing the points of my modified teeth.

"Good girl," he said at length, and stroked my hair back. Pausing to wrap long fingers around the back of my neck, he stood and brought me with him. "You have your orders," he said to the men. "Dismissed."

The walk to his office was rife with the sort of tension I'd never experienced before. Not when I watched my city fall, nor when flames swallowed my parents in a single greedy gulp.

Tension made all the worse when the door snapped shut, and he left me standing in the same spot I'd been whipped the night prior.

Wound too tight, a ball of anxiety sat heavy in my gut. Gooseflesh rising up, I tried to hide my body from eyes gone dark as pitch.

Because I knew.

My destiny didn't lie in sexual slavery to an entire garrison of Caledonian soldiers, but to the man who preferred to beat answers from a girl he thought helpless. Who meant to do a lot worse.

"How did you sleep?" he asked, jerking me from my thoughts.

Hands winding tighter about my ribs, I hid from his scrutiny. "I didn't."

He grinned, pacing circles around me. "You didn't *what*?"

"Sleep." I turned with him, uncomfortable exposing my back to a predator of this nature.

Something heavy pulsed between us, something wicked that tasted like gleeful victory, but he breathed an almost musical sigh. "I can see your time in the hole wasn't effective, as far as punishments go." He glanced toward the whips still decorating his desk. One eyebrow raised in contemplation.

Sweat bloomed on my skin, panic making me flush hot and cold all at once. My mistake realized too late. "Sir! I didn't sleep, *sir!*"

"Yesterday was a waste," he added as an afterthought. As if he hadn't heard my correction.

"Please," I whispered, hands raised. Breasts exposed, though I knew it was too late. Knew this trick wouldn't work twice now that he'd seen every piece of me. "I-I'm sorry, sir." I took a step toward his desk.

"Hob, if you touch one of those weapons, I'll introduce you to a whole new meaning of sorry."

I froze—the thought had barely formed in my mind.

"Come here," he said, voice a hard, unforgiving line. Promising things that drew an involuntary whimper from the back of my throat.

But my feet refused to move. "I—"

Seizing my bicep in a bruising grip, he pulled me toward the chains dangling from the ceiling.

"No!" I sobbed, and threw my weight in the opposite direction. Feet skidding across the worn hardwood floors. Knees locked. Fighting in the face of another punishment, for the thought of starting yesterday over was too much. "Please, I-I can't—"

"What you want isn't relevant," he said, turning as he led me to my doom. Lips curved around a smirk.

And without really meaning to, I snapped.

Lunging, I closed the distance between us with a

war cry and a single step. Punched that infuriating little grin with my free hand, with every spare ounce of strength I possessed.

At first, he did little more than grunt.

Didn't move or react beyond his head snapping to one side.

It wasn't until a breath hissed through his teeth that I realized what I'd done. *Who* I'd struck with a closed fist and no warning.

An unbound elite.

And I watched—one wrist still caught in a ring of clenched fingers—as he thumbed a drop of blood from his lower lip and frowned at the crimson smear. With every passing instant, his grip grew tighter and tighter, squeezing until the bones in my wrist ground together. Until a squeak of protest bubbled past my lips and drew his attention back to me.

Moving faster than I thought possible, he spun me. Wrenched one arm behind my back and folded me over the edge of his desk with a thump that stole my breath. Bare skin slapping against the polished surface, he forced me flat.

"Wait—"

A band of steel wrapped tight against my windpipe, cutting me off. Squeezing a warning that made my head spin.

His forearm, I knew, because an instant later, the full weight of his body fell across my back. Pinning me there, naked and exposed.

"Well, aren't we just full of surprises this morning?"

Already so far past the point of rescue, I tried to buck him off. "Get o—"

"Shut *up*," he snarled, and kicked my feet apart. Forcing my ankles wide as they might go, he filled the gap and made me feel every inch I never wanted to know.

Hard.

Breath hot against my ear, he shifted so I might feel the pulse of furious arousal when he set it to the most vulnerable piece of me. Leveraging a terrible threat, he pressed too close. Lips skating across my jawline, his breath tickled my ear an instant before his teeth found purchase on my left earlobe. Pinched.

A sob got caught in my chest, but I went still and small in his hands. Yielding to a predator far greater than myself.

"I'm going to enjoy breaking you very much," he whispered, and moved to stroke the vulnerable skin of my throat. Blunt fingernails leaving a trail of goose-flesh where he traced my pulse.

I squirmed, and felt him react *there*, too. Felt a kick between my legs that made me clench, eyes squeezed shut on a swell of shame.

"I've never trained a slave quite like you," he murmured, smiling against my cheek when I shivered.

Elite energy flared to life once more. Hunger with

a vengeance, darkness that beat against my senses, drawn to me without seeming to realize why.

"For most," he said, and released my trapped arm, leaving me free to brace with both palms, "this is a welcome reward." His fingers fell to my outer thigh, leaving a burning trail in the wake of so simple a gesture. "But not for you," he said. Edging up and over, rasping against tender skin no other had ever gotten close enough to touch, he claimed my hip and squeezed. Fingertips bit into the muscle, a ragged breath puffing against my cheek. "For you, this will be the worst kind of punishment."

And then, with an unforgiving grip, he pushed that flesh toward the desktop with relentless confidence. Spreading me in a lewd stretch, I was made to open for him. A band of male hardness notched into place with a roll of his hips, separated only by a bit of fabric. Held back by his zipper.

"Please," I whined, and it was the sound of defeat. "Don't do this. Set me free," I said, pleading. My voice hoarse. "You'd be out fifty dollars. For a slave n-no one even wants. Hardly worth mentioning."

"A valiant attempt, darling," he said, and laughed, a deep rumble that licked up the length of my spine. From tailbone all the way to the base of my skull. "But you've earned quite a reputation for causing trouble." He pushed into me hard enough that my hips bit the hardwood, then continued in a husky

whisper thick with malicious intent. "And, of course...
I can't just let you go..."

"The salt mines!" I gasped, tears blurring my
vision. "Let me die in the salt mines, *pl*—"

He hauled me up, my hips left pinned by that
unforgiving grip, tipped forward. My bottom spread
where he'd claimed a handful of muscle and fat.
Spine forced to bow when he straightened and took
me with him while his free hand snaked between my
breasts. Pausing to cup first the left, then the right, he
caught my nipple and bit my shoulder with a growl of
warning that rattled through my chest.

A gesture I could almost believe to be playful if it
weren't for that hand moving higher still. Palming my
throat, his fingers flirting with the notion of stran-
gling me.

Both hands flying to his wrist when he squeezed,
I writhed against his chest. Ground back and felt him
lurch where blunt heat was pressed to my core.

A deep groan spilled against my collarbone, and
he bore down. Hips picking up a heavy rhythm, he
thrust that thick length against me, grip tightening
on either side of my windpipe until I coughed.
Tugging on his wrist, desperate for a sip of air... my
entire body clenched with something I couldn't
name. Lower abs dancing as I tried to force my lungs
into submission and failed.

"That's it," he rumbled, gentle now. Guiding my
head to rest on his shoulder, he left my throat

stretched long and exposed. "Maybe it's the challenge," he murmured, abandoning my hip without giving anything away. "Or maybe it's just that you smell like innocence in a place where that's a bizarre rarity."

Eyes fixed to the ceiling, I shook my head, tears spilling over at last. Soaking my hairline as my breaths came ragged and harsh.

Long fingers spread across my belly, holding me tight.

But only for an instant.

His fingertips brushed the top of my mound, waxed bare and left utterly defenseless.

"N-*nooo*," I whispered, abandoning any effort to protect my airway in a desperate panic. Hands flying instead to stop him from taking the last shred of dignity I possessed.

"All I need is your name," he drawled, breathing against me. "Just one little compromise"—he kissed the corner of my lips, beard scruffy and rough against my ear—"and I won't make you come all over my fingers. Won't make you choke on my cock or swallow my come. You won't have to beg for it. I won't make you crawl. You can go back to the hole and sit in the dark. That's all I want," he whispered, and pushed a little... *lower*. To where I was hot and aching, poisoned with insidious elite energy. "Just your name..."

My *Tritan* name.

"I *can't*-can't remember—" Shaking my head, I sobbed and felt him shrug.

"Okay, then." Hardly bothering to notice when I hauled at his wrist with all my remaining strength, his touch slipped over tender skin and found me slick. Swollen. "Mmm," he groaned, and cupped my mound. "So wet for me."

Hiccupping, I shook my head. "N-No, I-I'm not, I can't—You don't—"

"Shh..." He spread my folds with two fingers, damning me with the creamy sound of my lie. Chuckling when I went stiff and hot with shame. "It's not your fault, pet." Another kiss, this one pressed to the back corner of my jaw. "Fear is a powerful motivator." He traced my seam with the point of his index finger, then moved back. Circling my clit. "An aphrodisiac for some women..."

Eyes wide, I shook my head.

"It's okay," he murmured. "I've got you." Catching that swollen bundle of nerves between the flat of his fingers, he circled once, then rolled it down the length of his digits. A lewd, slick track that let him reach through the mess to find my opening. Teasing me with the threat of plunging inside, only to pull back and do it all over again.

My knees buckled.

Shifting, he took my weight and rocked at my back. Hard and swollen, his energy a band of inflexible *want*. "It's agony, isn't it? Being so close..." Jaw working against my cheek, I felt him clench with that same brand of pain. "I could stop you here," he whispered, cupping my breast with his free hand. Picking up speed with the other. "Leave you hanging in more ways than one. Make you watch as I stroke my cock... until I paint this pretty little pussy with my come and leave you *dripping*... desperate for just... a little... *more*..."

My breath caught, and, head spinning, I started shaking.

"But you're going to come for me, aren't you? You're going to soak my fingers and come all over my hand. I can feel it. But it's okay," he said, speaking low against my ear. "I want you to come, pet. I want you to gush for me because I know you can't help it." He groaned, and shifting the bulk of his attention on my clit, he pinched my nipple.

Hard.

Lungs seizing, my back arched. An orgasm struck hard and fast, and I lurched forward to do exactly what he said. Hips jerking, I came at the command of a Caledonian elite with a silent sob.

Laid out on the desk, the wood warm and slippery beneath my heated skin, an oppressive silence fell over us. Penetrated only by the sound of ragged breathing, the occasional soft hiccup, my muscles went stiff as the fog lifted.

As I realized what I'd done.

Forehead pressed to the back of my neck, the

captain's cock was a brand against the ache he'd inspired. Throbbing with unspent fury, dark flames seethed at my back.

His voice laced with wicked amusement, he pressed another of those infuriating smirks to my throat and said, "Good girl."

And then he stepped back.

Watching me slip to the floor, a boneless puddle of wet, horrified misery, he reached for his cock. Adjusting himself, the front of his slacks glistened with the sheen of wetness.

Stained.

By *me*.

He took a step, a tempest ready to rage.

I flinched, hands coming up. Defensive, though I knew there was no escaping the second half of his threat. To make me swallow that girth. Beg for it. *Crawl.*

He reached over my head, pulled open a drawer, and rummaged through the contents, retrieving something that clanged when he set it down. Metal on wood.

Then, once more taking a knee, the captain pulled my hands away from my face with a touch that was as deadly as it was gentle. His thumb sweeping across my cheek, he brushed my tears away and gathered my hair away from my throat...

... so he could snap an iron collar around my neck.

9

———

Hooking one finger beneath the band of cold iron, I shifted the collar and scowled at the broad shoulders bunching and flexing before me. Eyes hot and dry, *itchy*, I watched him move without blinking. My gaze fixed to a beast until he produced a length of creamy blue satin and turned to face me once more.

"Up."

I bared my teeth.

The captain smirked and flicked the fabric out in a billowing curtain with a snap that made me recoil until I saw what it was he offered. A barrier held between us. The illusion of privacy.

"Up," he said again, and made a show of looking away. As if he hadn't already seen every part of me.

Touched.

Trembling, I did as he asked.

With a flourish, he swept the fabric over and around me. Wrapped me up from collarbones to ankles, but left my back exposed and the whiplashes on full display. Practiced fingers twisting in the material, he tied two ends together just below my breasts and again at my nape. Adjusting the flowing drapery until it swished with my every subtle movement, a waterfall of color both soothing and enticing.

My cheeks flushed hot. Fingers damp and twisting.

"Come along, Hob," he drawled, one large hand clamping high at the back of my neck as he led me from his office—the very same digits that had ravaged my pride and left me in ruins. Fingers so long they nearly touched at the front of my throat, his thumb playing with my pulse where it thrashed beneath my skin.

Betraying me.

The blunt edge of his nails teasing the fine hairs at the base of my skull, he guided me through the hall. His touch drawing up a wash of shivers that spilled down my back.

"Where are you taking me?" I asked, pleased that my voice held no hint of the mortified humiliation knifing through my guts.

He stooped without stopping, pressing close enough that his heat blistered my cheek, his arousal left unchecked. Still ravenous and unspent. "Now, now, Hob," he purred, breath a sweet and sinister fan.

A promise. "Wouldn't want to ruin the surprise, hmm?"

I licked my lips, fighting the urge to recoil. To hiss and spit against the unconscious display of elite strength.

"We're beginning your training today," he added, looming at my back. "And I have so many plans for you, but first, we need to do something about those teeth. Can't recoup my investment on a pleasure slave with only two useable holes..."

My breath caught, and with a rush of blood screaming in my ears, I began to sweat. At first, a bloom of heat, my face flushing a deep shade of red I could feel prickling into my hairline.

And then I went cold. All the way to my core. Teeth clenched hard enough to make my molars squeal, I swallowed back the urge to vomit all over the captain's clean wooden floors.

I had known slavery to the empire was a brutal life for females of any nation, but to stare into those inky depths and see my own undoing?

"You'll be trained for it, of course," he said, conversational as he reached over my shoulder to unlock his front door. "And I think you'll be surprised by just how much you can take. Even a skinny thing like you. Some of the men like to save some coin by sharing"—he shrugged—"which isn't to my taste, but I do applaud those frugal enough to overlook a rather tight fit..."

"I would rather d-die than—" A horrified sob burst free of my lips. "*P-please*, don't do this to me," I whispered and glanced up. Fell into eyes gone darker than pitch, and was ensnared by the wicked sparkle glimmering in those ebon depths.

Flames of elite energy billowed off his skin, a cruel lash of amusement. A predator toying with his next meal. "You'll be a *pleasure* slave, girl. When I'm done with you—"

"Captain!" Cam said, panting as he stumbled to a halt before us. Breathless and flushed. "You're needed on the front lines, sir. It's urgent. The general—"

"Report," the captain barked, and fingers tightening on my nape, he drove me into the street at a pace I couldn't match with any amount of ease. Made to take three steps for every one of his long-legged strides, my every stumbling step jarred my bones.

Murmuring in low tones, Cam spoke a string of militant gibberish I had no hope of understanding. Speaking of troop movements and the loss of "more fuckin' ground to those Eloran scum gurglers."

Bare feet slapping on the cobblestones, I staggered, caught up by the flowing skirts swirling around my ankles.

The captain made a sound at the back of his throat. "We'll have to put this off until tomorrow, Hob," he said, thrusting open a heavy iron door and ushered me through it. "I have to deal with your people," he murmured, his pace not slowing, even a little.

But although the kiss of elite energy lapped at the back of my skull, despite what it meant for any Elorans bold enough to stand against the empire, I was pleased. My secret was still mine, no matter how close I'd come to discovery.

I swallowed the smile, looking instead for a way to escape while the captain was occupied.

He'd brought me back to the bathhouse, but the room we entered was filled with women in all levels of undress. Each wore delicate bracelets and collars, lounging in heaps of pillows and silks. The air heavy with perfume and the high, tinkling laughter of female voices.

Pleasure slaves.

Upon our entry, several of the women squealed and rushed to greet the captain.

"My Lord Rawlings! How can this slave please you, sir?" a beautiful brunette asked, falling to her knees at his feet in a rush of transparent silk. Her nipples sparkled with tiny white gems, pebbled to draw the eye to where her flesh jiggled.

"I've missed you so much, sir! Allow me the honor of tending to your needs, I beg of you," said another with waist-length black hair.

Stomach churning, I pulled air through my teeth, straining not to smell the adoration these women had for a monster. Trained devotion.

And to my horror, women continued to simper and fawn, throwing themselves at his feet until we reached a raised dais piled high with pillows. A deep, wide bathing pool was situated in the room's heart, steam billowing off the heated surface.

"My Lord," said a beauty with eyes as green as Kyra's. Her look of quiet pride an immediate reminder of the woman who'd offered comfort while we'd been bound in Jasper's slave carriage. "Shall I have your private rooms prepared?"

The captain's fingers circled my throat, and he pushed my head against his shoulder. "Not today, Alicia. I have another chore for you."

"Anything," she breathed, watching him from beneath the fan of her lashes with a look that might only be described as coy.

Whether it was the murmur of pure subservience, the air thick with the stink of perfume, or the dazzling array of colored silks, I couldn't be sure. But I balked. Senses overloaded, I whined. Pushing against the captain's chest. My head thrown back, lips parted, I gasped, seeking a single breath not laced with the choking fog of adoration for this one man.

Strong arms circled my waist, a smirk pressed to my throat, he pulled me close. Chuckling as I thrashed, he said, "This is Hob," and turned me to face this cluster of females who would be my future. "She doesn't like people very much, but she's in desperate need of instruction."

"She's very pretty, my lord," Alicia said as she approached with a slow, seductive roll of full hips. Dainty fingers outstretched, she fingered a lock of my caramel locks.

Before I could lash out, the captain's grip on my neck forced me to remain still. Compliant to the silent warning.

"What other kind of training can we do, my lord?" she asked, her touch drifting past the iron collar to stroke the side of my breast.

Panic bubbled at the back of my throat, splashing with the acidic promise of rebellion that couldn't be helped. There was only so far he could push.

"Always eager, Alicia. But this one is mine to break. Mine to touch..." He led me to an ornate column in the center of the room and attached a chain to my collar, eliminating any hope of escape with a simple flick of nimble fingers. "If you raise a hand to anyone here," he murmured, knuckles tracing my cheek from temple to jaw, "I will toss you to my men and wash my hands of you. Understood?"

Blinking back tears, trembling where I stood before him, I nodded. "Yes, sir."

"Good. Cal?"

The soldier stepped into the fray. All steely, hard lines. "Sir?"

"See that she behaves," the captain drawled, holding eye contact as he backed toward the exit.

I watched him go. Watched until the door clanged

shut, and could only draw breath once separated from the swirling storm of elite energy. His fire gone from my senses, leaving me shivering in the cold.

Shock.

It settled into my blood, my bones. The trembling coming from so deep inside I wasn't sure it would ever ease.

"Where are you from?" the black-haired woman asked, a gentle smile tracing painted lips.

I could only stare at the spot where he'd last been. Bound to keep my temper, I held my tongue. I had no use for the company of women, for these soft creatures enslaved to their precious master, who offered a dedicated education in indoctrination.

"My name is Tala," she said as the rest gathered. "I've been with Captain Rawlings' company for over a year now. You'll like it here."

A musical sigh feathered against my ears. "The captain's just an amazing lover, isn't he?" asked a mousy girl I hadn't noticed, lounging in a pile of pillows and sipping from a ceramic cup.

"He hasn't touched her yet, Rabbit," Alicia said, flicking her a coil of hair over her shoulder. "They only brought her in yesterday. She's to learn the rules first. You remember how he is with the new ones. Pleasure is a *reward*," she said with a smirk, waggling her brows at the girls.

I felt the blood rush from my cheeks. Felt my skin

go white in a slow ooze of dawning horror. *"For you,"* he'd said, *"this will be the worst kind of punishment."*

Breath clogged in my throat, my lips sagged open. A low, rattling whine spilling over. Too quiet an implosion for any of the pleasure slaves to hear.

"Camille, how long did it take you to get her cleaned up?" Alicia asked, hands on hips. She regarded me with eyes that sparkled a warm, enticing green. Oblivious to the effect of her words. That I'd given Captain Asher Rawlings everything he asked for without any fight.

Because I couldn't help it.

"Three hours, but she didn't have *these* yesterday," Camille said from behind me, touching the tender lash marks on my back.

Teeth bared, I spun to face her and found myself in the middle of a loose circle with no way out. The chain keeping me in place growing heavier than I could bear to carry for much longer.

"What did you do to deserve a whipping?" Camille asked with wide eyes.

"So *this* is the wild one," Alicia whispered, her tone melodic as if connecting dots. "The one who was freeing slaves." Circling me, she took her turn, peering at my back. Fingers pressed to the spot just beneath her lips, she clapped her hands and said, "Too long spent running from the empire, I think. But we can show her what it's like to live in comfort, can't we ladies?"

With a thump, my knees hit the tiles. A sparkle of pain that should have been enough to shake me free of this spiral into darkness, but wasn't.

Not even close.

"Give her room to breathe," Alicia said from a blurry distance, shooing them all away. Skirts tucked, she claimed the spot on my right side. Her back pressed to the column, she wriggled close to my side. Draping her arm about my shoulders, she offered the comfort of touch I couldn't deny on the threat of gang rape and an uglier death. A gift of courage from a pleasure slave, her energy bolstered my tolerance and left me worn thin and ragged. "It's okay," she whispered, tucking a lock of sweaty hair behind my ear. "This life is overwhelming, at first, but you'll come to like it here. We're a family. The only ones we've got left."

A derisive snort burst from my nostrils, but that was all I could muster.

She squeezed me. "You'll see."

10

The rest of the day was spent lurking on the outskirts. Chained in place, watching. Being watched, for Cal had maintained his vigil in the captain's absence. But after the initial excitement, the pleasure slaves—at least—left me in peace.

Except for Alicia.

Chattering nonstop, she continued to hover, persisted in trying to draw me into meaningless conversation as she plied me with sweet cakes and tea.

I touched nothing. Inspecting the food and drink with a skeptical eye.

With a placid, knowing smile, Alicia brought her latest offering to her own lips. Took a sip, then pressed the warm ceramic into my palms. "Try it," she said. "It soothes the nerves like nothing else."

After a moment, I nodded. Took a sip that helped to ease the lump of curdled shame lodged in my throat.

"I've been here for..." She laughed, shaking her head, one hand skating over and through her glossy mane. "Years, I think. I stopped counting after a time. And you know," she said, the glittering green of her gaze pulling me in, "accepting it? This life? Made it a *lot* easier. I have a certain type of power here. Influence over men like Captain Asher Rawlings." She grinned, flashing the sharp edge of slightly crooked teeth.

My eyes fell to my lap, to the empty cup. And blinking away a fog of hated moisture, I rolled the ceramic between my palms. Fingers stiff. Outstretched.

"He can be... *intense*," she said softly, fishing for something deeper. Something I couldn't give her. Couldn't even give myself. "But once you learn the rules—"

"I have to pee," I said, voice a ragged thing that scraped over my vocal cords.

"Oh!" She stood in a rush, then clapped her hands and offered to help me to my feet. "I'll take you. You're going to *love* this. We have private baths. Luxury I never saw before coming here."

Ignoring her outstretched hand, I stood under my own power. Tinkling chains all I needed to illuminate my inability to leave the spot where the captain had left me.

"Ah, okay. Just... give me a moment. Cal!" she called, and turned in a sweep of swirling silks, but a moment later, the distant rumble of approaching feet could be heard. "Shit," she breathed, chewing at her lower lip. "Shift change."

The doors burst open to admit a small crowd of soldiers. Many faces I recognized from the captain's hall this morning. Many more I didn't. All seeking the comfort of the women who stood in a rush of perfumed opulence, cooing in welcome.

Slipping around the column, I shifted into darkness to watch. Sickened, yet fascinated. Not by the men, who were crude and obvious in their sordid desires, but the *women*. Their energy sparkled with a particular blend of eagerness and want, yet was laced with something much more... sinister.

Greed.

"This is all the power they have," Alicia breathed, appearing at my side. She watched with me as some of the women pulled men into private rooms while others went to work right there in plain sight. Amid pillows and onlookers, they were utterly shameless in their eagerness to undress. "Come," Alicia said, and touched my elbow. "I have the key."

She unlocked my collar. Freed me from the column.

I didn't move.

Eyes flicking left to right, searching for an exit I might take before any could stop me.

"Don't," Cal warned, his dark eyes narrowed. One hand drifting to his belt, where a weapon was holstered.

My lip curled, but without argument, I allowed Alicia to lead me into the powder room and left Cal standing just outside the door of a windowless room with only one exit.

Six latrines were set on a single, high bench made of polished marble, each separated by a privacy wall. Secluded by mellow orange curtains.

Without pausing to admire the obscene luxury, I claimed the one furthest from the door. Jerked the curtain closed behind me, hiked my skirts, and sat, taking the first full breath of relative privacy I'd had since my arrival.

"Use the cloths to pat yourself dry, unless"—Alicia cleared her throat—"your business is... well." She laughed. "There's a pot of warm soapy water there if you need it."

Cheeks burning, my lips parted on a condescending snarl that died in my throat when I saw the offerings she referenced. The pleasure slaves used actual soft fabric to clean themselves—a far cry from the leaves and moss I'd grown accustomed to over the years, and one that made me feel every bit the uncultured wild thing instead of the Tritan lady I'd once been.

I finished with my affairs without a word, as if I used fine cloth for such business every day.

And when I stepped clear of the curtain, Alicia was there, waiting.

"Are you the one who's been freeing slaves?" she whispered, a soft breath of sound that hardly dared to touch my ears, let alone travel from this room.

Eyes flicking to the door, I hesitated. Unwilling to trust this woman who boasted of her influence over men like Captain Asher Rawlings. Of her position earned on her back, a traitor to the very people I'd risked everything to free.

"Please," she hissed, green eyes sparkling with the first hint of something earnest I'd seen from her. The act fell away. "I just need to know if my daughter... if she... if she made it."

I swallowed the rising lump because... just as with Jake and his tattered little family, Alicia was surviving. Using any tool she had to do it, and, for that, I couldn't blame her without also judging myself. And so, with a tight nod, I acknowledged my role in sending refugees across the ocean.

Alicia's lips went white around a slow whistle of held breath. "She had my eyes," she began. "My hair, and—"

"Kyra?" I asked, a horrible sense of gloom spreading through my chest.

Alicia blinked, just once, before she said, "We called her... Katrina."

"I... I'm sorry," I whispered, glancing again at the door. Leery of revealing my accent, but to reunite Kyra with her mother? "We were captured together."

Folded hands clapped over Alicia's throat, practiced and elegant, as if to keep a sob of grief locked away where none might hear it. "Then I'll see her soon," she breathed, as artful tears gathered on her lashes. Making her eyes sparkle in a way I couldn't help but empathize with, for it reflected my own deep well of grief. Loss. "That's... that's something."

"I'm sorry." I took a breath, hypnotized by the things playing across her beautiful face that looked so much like the girl who'd offered me comfort in a place barren of such things. And then, I placed an awkward hand on Alicia's forearm. "I didn't get the chance to save her, but"—I licked lips gone dry and bloodless—"but if you can help me escape, Alicia, I can help *so many* others. Your people. Your family. Please..." My grin tightened in a desperate bid to make myself heard, clinging to the only woman who might be capable of helping me evade a fate far worse than a life of spread thighs and unwanted orgasms.

For a long moment, Alicia was quiet. Her pulse thrashing at the base of her throat the only hint I could see that promised she was considering my words. Her energy a swirling mess of conflict and hesitation laced with something I couldn't name.

And then, "I can get you free, sister. Soon, if we're lucky." She smiled, then. And it was beautiful. An invitation to trust I couldn't quite reject. "What's your name?"

My breath caught. Tears flooding my lashes, I choked on a sob. "Mila," I said, giving up my name for the first time since Josh had betrayed me to save his dirty, starving children. "My name is Mila."

Green eyes went wide, ringed in white. "You're Tritan," she said, hardly bothering to whisper.

My eyes flicked back to the door, and I hushed her. Hissing through bared and pointed teeth.

"That's why you don't speak. Your accent."

I nodded, throat tight. Jaw flexing.

"And your hair..." Deep in thought, she fingered a caramel lock.

"It's a dye," I whispered. "A stain made from walnuts. And I don't think it can hold up to another shampooing..."

Alicia nodded, then said, "If he finds out, you'll be the jewel of this harem." It was a statement spoken without jealousy or spite. "A prize unmatched."

A squeal escaped my throat, one that evoked the nauseating imagery the captain had painted before leaving me here. All my holes used, shared between men happy to buy my time. My body. "Alicia, *please*," I whispered, my voice splintering with urgency. "When can we leave?"

The pleasure slave smoothed her palms down her skirts. Swallowing twice, a frown pinched between her brows. "I have to make arrangements," she said, then squeezed my shoulders. "But be ready. *Tonight.*"

11

———————

"Patience, sister," Alicia whispered, and chained me to the marble column once more. Leaving me alone with Cal and a room full of men fixated on satisfying their carnal appetites. "I won't be long."

Heart pounding, I nodded. Helpless to do anything but watch her go.

Spine pressed to the cold stone, I settled in to wait. Ignoring the grumble of my stomach, the aching skin of my back, and the sensual energy whipping at my stunted priestess senses. Refusing to so much as lift my gaze from where it had fallen into my lap. Couldn't bear to count the men each of the pleasure slaves serviced, and whenever the captain's inky black gaze shimmered at the edges of my memory, I shook him away with clenched teeth and palms.

I did nothing to draw attention to myself. Didn't

so much as uncross my legs or sigh at an audible decibel.

It wasn't until the men began to filter out, one-by-one, that I dared watch them go. Grew bold enough to taste that they were leaving tired and deplete.

The same was true for the pleasure slaves. All of them took turns lounging in the steaming bath, soaking away the pains of their work. Bathing each other with fragrant soaps, only to smear yards of naked flesh with oils and scented creams.

And still, Alicia hadn't returned.

"Well, well, well," said a voice I knew. One that made me lurch in hated recognition. "What have we here?"

Beau.

Wearing a simple wrap that revealed little of her aging skin, her face was swollen and bruised—purple around her left eye where the imprint of my knuckles could be seen with startling ease.

Instead of an apology, I offered a savage flash of teeth, admiring my work.

"Beau, what happened?" Tala exclaimed, rushing to her side.

The matronly woman returned my smile, though hers was cold and cruel. "Keep your distance from *that one*, girls."

"Goodness!" Tala murmured, inspecting the damage. "*She* did this? But, why?"

"Because she's a no good, vicious animal," Beau

hissed through a sneer. "No idea why the master is bothering with her at all. Should toss her to the other animals in the dungeons with her kind."

"Ah," Tala hummed. "Well, the transition isn't... easy for all of us, is it?"

I glanced at the door, seeking Alicia's return.

"Get her up," Beau snapped, flicking her wrist at my face in a way that made her arm jiggle.

Cal unclipped my chain from the wall, wrapped the extra length about his wrist to be used as a leash, then stooped. One hand on my bicep, he hauled me to my feet.

But I didn't fight them. Instead, my eyes fell to the polished tiles once more, being led on a leash without a fight. Counting down the minutes until Alicia returned with my exit.

It wasn't until my feet hit a set of stone steps that I bothered to lift my gaze.

The bathing pool.

I balked.

"N-no," I rasped, trying to tug my elbow out of Cal's grip. "I had a bath yesterd—"

Beau sneered, the expression twisting her face into something polluted and ugly. "Daily bathing is a requirement, you filthy little beast. Captain's orders."

Bracing, I shook my head. "No."

"Come now," Tala hummed, trying to soothe. "The water is warm. It's a *luxury*, sister. Especially

considering how many men are in Captain Rawlings'
company."

Feminine laughter rang out, echoing off the walls,
but I twisted. Eyes seeking the place I'd last seen
Alicia as panic began to bubble in my chest. "Please,
don't—"

A large hand landed between my shoulder
blades. With a shove, Cal sent me tumbling over the
edge of the pool.

Knees skinned, I went in head-first. Caught
myself just before I face-planted into an underwater
bench, then came up spluttering with indignant rage
only to be jerked to the edge by my neck. The chains
in Cal's hands were nothing more than leverage, an
advantage he flouted at a whim.

I coughed, scrubbing water from my eyes. Trying
to catch my reflection in the rippling surface,
desperate to see if the dye was running. My disguise
slipping away as I stood in waist-deep water.

"Hold her still," Beau said. And, with a wicked
gleam in her milky eyes, she produced that accursed
soap, slathering it between palms gnarled with age.

Cal yanked on the leash, threatening to hang me
should I fight.

Head tipped back, I shivered in the over-warm
bath. Felt the old woman's claws score my scalp as she
worked the soap into my hair hard enough to tear the
follicles loose.

But I didn't make a sound of protest.

Didn't so much as wince at the tearing pain.

I merely dug my nails into my palms and counted the seconds, awaiting Alicia's return.

Without warning, a bucket of warm water sloshed over my head, ringing my hair and sending soap cascading into my eyes and mouth as it ran all down my front.

"How could there possibly be more filth in that hair of yours?" Tala asked, running a hand through the cloudy water swirling around my waist.

A strangled sob burst from my lips, but that was it.

Alicia wouldn't be much longer.

She wouldn't.

And then Beau said, "Again," lathering yet more of her infernal suds into a froth before she slapped it atop my head.

"I-isn't it clean enough?" I begged, hating the wet slide of tears mixing with the dirty water tracking down my face. Already, my hair was several shades lighter.

A third shampooing would be my undoing.

And Alicia wasn't here.

"You're unfit for the privilege of Captain Rawlings' company," Beau replied acidly.

"It's only soap," Tala said. "It can't hurt you."

At this, I laughed. And—with a slipping sense of reality—had to admit Beau's malevolent scalp massage actually felt rather nice.

"What do you think of red silks with her pale skin tone?" someone asked, though I couldn't be bothered to pin the voice to the face. "The captain favors the darker tones, but red would look *so* pretty."

I knew the instant it happened.

The very moment Beau learned my secret.

Her energy, which had been a dull, monotonous hum of little significance, sparkled to life. Shocked, her hands went still in the bubbles crowning my head.

"Beau, *please*," I said, making no effort to mask my Tritan accent, unable to bear another glance at the door where Alicia *wasn't*. "You hate me, don't you?" I laughed, but it was a hopeless sound laced with grief. "Now is your chance to be rid of me f-forever."

"Leave us!" she barked, and for a moment, the pleasure slaves stood in a ring of shocked silence. Oblivious to the revelations unfolding before them. And then, "Go!" Beau shrieked.

They fled, abandoning us without further questions.

Trained to obey.

Only Cal remained. Silent. Holding my leash, protecting Beau from the dangerous creature wearing a muddy disguise that couldn't stand up to a little soapy water.

"Please," I whispered and hiccupped. My gaze fixed to the ceiling. "I can't be a slave."

Beau pulled her gnarled fingers from my hair,

gathered a bucket of warm water, and rinsed the suds away.

"Holy *shit*," Cal whispered as my heritage was revealed. Silver-blonde hair floated in the murky water, exposed for the first time in years.

The door banged open.

But I didn't bother to look.

Too late.

She'd come back too late to help.

"*Oh*," Alicia breathed, arriving at last.

I squeezed my eyes shut, for there was nothing else to say.

Nothing to be done that could undo this discovery.

And as my senses sparkled with the kiss of dark flames, drawn to the approaching storm of volatile, elite energy, I wished for the training to become a pleasure slave. To spread my legs in service to the empire instead of the alternative.

The doors opened once more, and this time, I couldn't seem to stop myself. Watching through the eyes of another, I turned my head and found the very last face I wanted to see when I was soaking wet. My every modest curve on lewd display. Nipples pebbled tight with a cold wash of fear.

"Lord Rawlings!" Beau called and dumped another bucket of water over my head, rinsing away the very last of my flimsy trickery. "Sir, you must come! See for yourself."

The captain didn't hesitate. Crossing the distance between us with sure steps, fingers flicking the buttons at his wrists, he rolled his sleeves back. Never so much as blinking away from my watery gaze. Feasting on the horror written all over my face.

With every step closer, the tempest brewing in his bottomless glare darkened. Lashing at me with a thing I didn't recognize.

At first.

But when he was close enough to touch my lips with the pad of his thumb, I knew.

It was *hunger.*

"I-I'm sorry, sir. I meant for the discovery to be yours," Beau said with a bow, stepping clear.

For several long moments, I was breathless. Sick with anticipation.

"What is your name?" he asked at last, running gentle fingers through my hair. His dark gaze torn from my face to watch the white ends flutter in the water.

My lips parted on a ragged sob, a choked hiccup. But nothing else came out.

He hushed me, then. Cupping the back of my neck with one hand, brushing his first two fingers over my lips with the other. "I want to hear you say it."

"Mila," I whispered because all hope was lost.

"*Mila*," he said, dipping closer to my face. Pressing his forehead to mine, he took a deep breath and exhaled gleeful victory. "Such a beautiful *Tritan* name."

"Just let me go," I whispered, tears making my voice nearly unrecognizable.

He hummed, kissed the corner of my lips, and pulled me to the edge of the pool. "No. I think not." And then, heedless of his crisp uniform, the captain hauled my limp body from the water, sloshing murky liquid all over the floor.

Holding me tight against his chest.

"Alicia," he drawled, squeezing the remaining water from my hair.

She stepped forward, eyes downcast. Her face etched with a heavy sadness. "Sir?"

When the captain turned to face her, a truly depraved smile spread across his lips. "Well done."

I jerked in his arms, my every limb flinching at those two measly syllables.

Turning, my chest tight and hot with the first flickering flames of hatred bursting to life in my chest, I met Alicia's glimmering green eyes.

And saw the truth.

"*Traitor*," I breathed, the word slipping through clenched teeth with a venomous hiss. "You've killed me. I trusted you," I said, voice rising on a tide of pure, unfiltered loathing.

Alicia's face twisted. Brow pinched, she looked as if she'd swallowed something sour. "Mila—"

Scowling, tears drying up, an animal snarl rattled

between my modified canines. "I *trusted* you," I spat. "And you delivered me into the hands of an *elite*."

At this, the captain began to laugh. Low and deep. Extinguishing my rage, he flooded my veins with elation. His hands grew tight and possessive in a way that sent my pulse hammering behind my eyes. Confused when his energy licked out, igniting in my very blood. Simmering at first before it became a triumphant, rolling boil. An all-consuming surge of victory that rendered me silent.

Struck dumb by his might.

"Oh, *Mila*," he whispered, then turned. Carried me to a couch piled high with pillows. A dirty thing where I'd seen men expose themselves to pleasure slaves who knelt between their spread thighs. Choking and slurping in an obscene show.

Unconcerned with the sticky mess or that I was soaking wet and shivering in his arms, he sat, arranging me across his lap. My back pressed to the arm of the couch, legs draped over his thighs.

"I should have known," he murmured, unable to peel his eyes from my face. Not bothering to hide the ravenous edge of his mirth. "I mean, how else could you have evaded the empire for so long? Freeing slaves... attacking trained soldiers, *surviving* through the winter. It's absurd," he said, and his low chuckle rumbled straight through my ribs and into my lungs. "Unless, of course, there was something *other* about you. Something... special." He grinned, gathered my sopping wet hair in careful fingers, then tugged it to the side. Exposing my neck. The collar he'd shackled me with just that morning.

"I'm not special," I whispered, but couldn't look away. "Just lucky."

"Then how," he drawled, and worked the latch on the iron collar, "did you know I'm an elite?" The collar fell with a clink.

Ears ringing, I could only shake my head, staring into the seething void behind his pupils.

My doom.

"Say it, Mila. Tell them what a prize you really are."

"I'm Tritan—"

He cupped my face with a large, calloused hand. Thumb moving to peel back my bottom lip, exposing my modified canines. "These are a rather obvious tell. Only a priestess could do such a thing—and a powerful one at that."

My eyes widened—I had no training in my craft and only a basic understanding of how it all worked. But if I were wrong...

I could turn the tide of the war.

In favor of the Caledonian Empire.

"There's a simple test," the captain said, and flung his outstretched hand in the traitor's direction. Snapping long, almost elegant fingers. "Alicia."

Without a word, she dropped a simple box into his palm and stepped back. Her face wiped clear of any theatrical emotion. Wooden, like the empire puppet she was.

The captain flicked the latch on the box with his left hand, then withdrew a masculine-looking gold cuff. It was unadorned by jewels but otherwise a perfect match to the one I had seen General Tilcot wearing.

He set it aside, and, with much more care, removed two small golden bracelets. The last thing in the box was a collar with a small glass vial embedded in the gold.

"Here's how this works," the captain said. "If I snap these bracelets on your wrists and you're absent priestess blood, they are nothing more than pretty golden circlets. If not... well... they'll bind us together forever."

"Don't... don't do this to me."

Ignoring me, the captain plunged his free hand between us, rummaged around, then drew a knife. "The bond requires a blood exchange, you see. My elite blood will activate the chains, and yours will seal them."

He drew a confident line across the exposed skin at his wrists, opening his flesh. Fumbling with the feminine collar, he popped the tiny glass vile with his thumbnail and set the opening to the blood welling against bronzed skin.

All four pieces of jewelry glowed an intense white

for a moment before returning to their original golden hue.

"I understand the bond is quite painful at first, and for that, I'm sorry." He shrugged, adjusting me on his lap so I could feel the hard length of his arousal beating against my outer thigh. "Can't be helped."

Watching as if from above, I was listless, floating on an ocean of complete horror. Unable to so much as lift a hand against him.

Not even when he stroked the delicate column of my throat, drawing up a bubble of fresh terror.

"Ready?" he asked with a smile, and snapped the collar around my neck. Plucking first my left, and then my right, wrist off my belly, he snapped the manacles in place.

Bracing for the pain, I went stiff. Eyes squeezed shut.

Nothing happened.

A snort of laughter churned up from my gut and I grinned, lightheaded, holding out my wrists. "Didn't work."

"Beautiful, Mila," he cooed. "Didn't I tell you the bond needs a *blood exchange*?" He snatched my outstretched wrist and pressed the tip of his blade into my skin. Making a small cut before repeating the ritual, he filled the vial in the masculine cuff with my blood.

It lit up like the others had, emitting a blinding flash of white.

"*Beautiful*," he whispered, but this time, the light didn't fade.

Not until he snapped it closed on his own wrist.

Fire erupted where the gold touched my skin—wrists and throat—and I screamed. Startled from my lethargy as molten agony lit into my flesh.

Metal burned through my skin and bones and in a matter of moments, I would certainly be dead.

Yet, on my next raspy breath, the pain ceased. Gone in an instant as if it had never been at all, leaving me trembling in the captain's arms. Wrapped tight, my head lolling back, tears streaking unchecked down heated cheeks.

But everything was different.

Changed on a fundamental level.

And then the air stilled in my lungs as I became aware of my proximity to a magnificent pillar of strength.

Greater than anything I'd ever sensed.

I dragged my head up and fell into his gaze.

Captain Asher Rawlings, elite soldier of the Caledonian Empire, was now bound to a priestess of considerable power.

Me.

I sobbed, rubbing at the lingering pain in my wrists and throat, unable to fight when he cradled me against his chest. Utterly without hope, for I was trapped.

Forever.

"Shh, Mila, shh," he whispered, scooping me up and stroking my hair. Tucking me beneath his chin. "It's over now, pet."

"I hate you," I said before succumbing to the sweet release of darkness.

Thank you for reading *Flame to Frost, The Last Tritan*, book I. Flip the page for a full chapter preview of book II, *Frost to Dust*!

If you like *free things, sneak peaks, giveaways, and super secret news about future projects*, then boiii is there a place for you! Tis called The Daniverse, and you can join by searching for "The Daniverse, by Myra Danvers" on Facebook.

FROST TO DUST

A dense fog swirled between my ears. Echoing with a distant call to wake, yet mocking my every effort to obey. In my wrists and throat, a lingering ache gnawing at my sinew. Pressing burning kisses to the hurt.

And through it all, white-hot flames lit the dark. Calling me back.

Demanding my return.

When at last I was able to peel my lids apart, it was to find I was curled around myself on a couch, fully dressed. Clad in a black knee-length wrap. Knotted behind my neck, my back left bare all the way to the top of my bottom. Exposed to the chill of a darkened room.

How I had come to be this way, I could not recall.

Blinking, groggy and disoriented, I brushed at the hair sticking to my sweaty brow.

A flash of gold caught my attention.

Manacles.

On *my* skin.

Horror bled through my veins with the return of memory, and with a cry, I clawed at the warm gold only to recoil in pain.

They were deep. The seam between gold and flesh utterly indiscernible, as if melted into my skin. Buried into the meat in such a way that I knew they might never be removed.

"Nooo," I moaned, voice trembling, gaze transfixed to what I couldn't change. There would be no chafing, no getting snagged on clothing, and no itching beneath the gold.

A smooth, cultured chuckle skated across my nape, making me whirl where I sat, fists raised.

"They're quite permanent," the captain said, dark eyes two gleaming pricks of light that watched from across a darkened room. Cruel amusement etched into every line of his face.

I gasped.

Naked from the waist up, hair still damp from the bathhouse—tousled and unruly—his lower half was encased in dark slacks. Muscle rippled as he fidgeted with a length of fabric, watching me without so much as a blink.

"Where am I?" I asked through dry lips.

"We are in the master bedroom of the house I occupy, in what used to be Elora," he replied, closing the distance between us with a slow, relentless roll of his hips.

Heat flared across my cheeks. "Don't touch me," I hissed, and pressed my back to the couch.

He hummed through a smirk. "Ah, but I own you, Mila. It is my right to do whatever I damn well please with my property."

"You don't own me," I snapped, baring teeth. Braced for the invasion of my personal space. Straining *not* to see the shape of long fingers, to remember the press and slide—

"Mmm," he purred, stepping too close. Enough that his heat touched my collarbones. "And *that* sounds like a challenge."

"It shouldn't," I hissed, and hopped onto the back of the couch. Crouched at eye level, knuckles white—until he straightened, towering above me.

"Such a saucy mouth," he crooned, grinning now. "I can think of plenty of things to keep those pretty lips of yours busy."

In response, I merely showed him my teeth. A silent dare for him to put something delicate in my mouth.

He lunged for my arm with a bark of cold laughter, but I was ready.

Throwing my weight in the opposite direction, I made a beeline for the door.

"Oh, Mila?" he sang, and in an instant, my every muscle seized stiff and solid against my will.

A fine tremor rippled through my body, but no matter how hard I tried to struggle—to fight or flee—I was frozen.

In my wrists and throat, a burning tingle that tasted of dark flames. Ravenous, burning frost that buried pointed teeth deep into my marrow and supped on my life force. Gulped down great, heaving swallows of my energy before I had a chance to do more than sense it going to support another.

Stolen.

Warm fingers skated down the length of my exposed spine. Bumping over the ridges—a shiver the only movement I was allowed.

His voice was a soft, cultured hum of debauchery and threat when he asked, "Would you like to learn why your cuffs are called '*Tritan chains*' when there are no chains in sight?"

With my back to the captain, I hadn't a choice but to stand utterly still. Held perfectly immobile, he left me trembling in the center of his bedroom, my body no longer mine to control. Jaw locked tight, for his question was rhetorical.

"Look at your wrists for me, darling."

My head bowed and my gaze dropped, and though I tried with all my might to deny the command, I couldn't help but look.

Glowing.

Bright light burning without heat, the cuffs encircling my wrist were blazing with a brilliance that made my eyes water. But it wasn't the complete inability to move, nor the threat of what the captain might do with this absolute control.

It was my skin.

Standing rigid beneath the surface, tracing a handspan away from the manacles, my veins were illuminated with the pulse of molten gold.

Asher, infecting my very blood with his tainted, Caledonian influence.

He stepped around me, strolling into my line of vision. "Beautiful, isn't it?" he asked, and dragged the back of his knuckles down my cheek. And then, with a ravenous smirk, he lifted his wrist to show off the matching cuff fused to his skin. A golden circlet glowing with *my* energy. "They allow me to control you," he murmured. "I can stop you from running with nothing more than a thought." One finger on my chest, he pushed me back. "I can have you drop to your knees and worship my cock like a seasoned whore," he continued, herding me toward the couch against my will. "And I can make you like it, though"—he smirked—"that comes from experience, not the chains."

Panic bubbled up between my ribs, and as if he wanted to hear the desperation in my voice, he released my jaw enough to allow me to say, "Please don't," in scarcely more than a whisper. Shamed into begging.

Into being *allowed* to beg.

A laugh bubbled up from deep inside his chest, and he said, "Sit," through that vile smirk that only widened when I obeyed without a moment's hesitation. "Believe me, pet," he drawled, and slid one hand up, around the curve of my hip and beneath the cushion—under the scraps of black silk—to cup the sensitive meat of my bottom. "You'll beg. And it will be beautiful."

Head falling back, I spat, "I won't beg to be raped," through pointed teeth. Letting him feel every bit of my hatred. My helpless wrath.

He watched as my thighs fell apart at the slightest, coaxing touch, then settled between them. One knee pressing against my core, he stooped. Pressed his lips to my neck, teeth rasping over throbbing, delicate flesh. "Do you think the pleasure slaves throw themselves at my feet because I abuse them?" he whispered against my ear, and sent ice shivering through my blood. "Because I force them?"

But in spite of myself, I sneered. Goaded into bickering, despite the way my heart hammered behind my ribs. "You're right. A good whipping really is the best way to a woman's heart."

A wicked grin flicked against the corner of my jaw. "Your heart holds no interest to me, slave," he murmured, and set his knee to rock against the place where I ached. "And I already have what I *need* from you."

"I'll die before I service you or your men," I

snarled, trapped beneath him. Unable to so much as lift a finger against his influence. Helpless to the whims of cruelty or mercy. Tormented by the wicked lust flickering in those inky, Caledonian eyes.

Amusement lapped at my senses. Foreign and dark and obliterating my indignant fury, he possessed me. Completely. Filled me with elite energy and left me gasping and disoriented. "You belong to me now, Mila. And I don't share."

Tears flooded my lash line, but I clung to the only thing I had left. Snark. "Says the man with a harem of public sex slaves."

"Purchased for the men I command."

"That's the very definition of sharing!"

He laughed before pressing his lips to mine. Stealing my breath, my voice. Every last drop of my sense.

"What I mean to say is that I shall not be sharing *you*." His influence faded away before I could muster a response, leaving me free to squirm. To fight with more than words and wit. "Come," he said, and pushed off the couch, retreating into an ensuite bathroom without a backward glance. "We'll be late for supper."

I scrubbed at my arms, my throat and wrists, trying to shake the feeling of Captain Asher Rawlings crawling through my blood and sinew. Learning everything that I was from the inside out. And, voice shaking, I said, "I'm not hungry," through a curled lip.

"And I wasn't asking."

He reappeared, wearing a black suit that hugged his muscular frame. Glittering with the stars and pins that denoted his rank within the Caledonian army. For a moment, he simply took me in. Dark eyes narrowed, flicking over my clenched fists, my spread, braced feet. And then, "Don't spoil my good mood with a fight you can't win, Mila. I can promise you won't like the consequences."

I laughed, despite the tears fogging my vision. "What more can you do to me? You can't kill me—I'm the source of your newfound power. Probably the very last free priestess, which means you'll *never* have another chance like this," I said, gaining confidence with every spoken word. Enough that I dared stalk toward him in my temper. "I can heal any damage you do to my body because I no longer have anything to hide. So go ahead. You can't hurt me, *elite*."

For the space of several breaths, there was nothing. Only the quiet sounds of a one-sided power struggle.

And then, "That you think so is oddly... refreshing. The opinion of a sheltered, naive little girl, of course, but refreshing nevertheless. And tempting as it might be to teach you the errors in your thinking, I'm due at General Tilcot's manse at the top of the hour." He paused then, fidgeting with a golden button at his wrist, shaking his head as if amused by my passion. "Let me offer you some advice, given that

I'm in something of a celebratory mood. Go out of your way to behave yourself in the company of these men. Under no circumstances are you to draw attention to yourself, do you understand me?"

I laughed, sneering. "Will my bad behavior reflect poorly on you?" I cooed, lightheaded with the rush of being near such a villain. The deadly push and pull I wasn't sure I'd survive. Wasn't sure I could muster the effort to care, given all I'd lost.

One large, rough hand settled on the back of my neck, and I was made to still as he caught my gaze in the bottomless, inky swirl of dark eyes. He said, "Yes," in such a way that saw my snide retort whither on my tongue. Held rapt and attentive. "Owning a priestess is a privilege. One that can be taken away without impacting my status as an asset to the empire."

It was my turn to grin, and I let him see the savage point of my teeth. "So I *can* be rid of you, then? I can break this infernal bond and—"

"You mistake me," he said, and closed what little distance there was between us. Chest to chest, looming above me in a way that made me feel tiny. Fragile and insignificant. "I don't need to be *in possession* of my priestess to be an asset to the empire. That is, to use your power to kill rebel scum." He cupped the back of my neck and let a rough thumb skate over my cheek, beneath my eye before his fingers tangled in the fine hairs at my nape. "They can hide any embarrassing assets away in the capital. Locked away in a cell, where no one will ever think to wonder after your health. Where it doesn't matter that you're bound to me, or that I have no intention of sharing that sweet little pussy with a garrison of my men." His fingers grew tight with warning. "There are things you've never thought to be terrified of, Mila. Horrible things that would see you begging to take my cock. To please me in any way your pretty little head can dream up, for nothing at all, except the promise that you'll remain in *my* care. So *yes,* Mila. Your bad behavior will reflect poorly on me, but *you* will pay the higher price." He released me, then. Took a quick breath and stepped back, raking one hand through thick, dark hair. "But there's only one way to break this bond."

"A-and what's"—I cleared my throat—"What's that?"

He shrugged, dark eyes glittering and heavy with warning. "You'll have to die."

***

Grab your copy of Frost to Dust today!

Atom and Evil

- Delirium, Atom and Evil, Book I

MYRA DANVERS

USA Today Bestselling author, Myra Danvers, is best known for her compelling mix of unique science fiction and dark fantasy worlds that feature feisty heroines, antihero men, and of course, proper villains. Though you may not always know who is who until the final pages...

facebook.com/MyraDanvers

instagram.com/myradanvers

bookbub.com/profile/myra-danvers

goodreads.com/MyraDanvers

www.ingramcontent.com/pod-product-compliance
Lightning Source LLC
Chambersburg PA
CBHW051231210726
48290CB00003B/899